ASKING FOR TROUBLE

By
Alex McAnders

McAnders Books

*****

The characters and events in this book are fictitious. Any similarity to real persons, living or dead, is coincidental and not intended by the author. The person or people depicted on the cover are models and are in no way associated with the creation, content, or subject matter of this book.

All rights reserved. No part of this book may be reproduced in any form or by any electronic or mechanical means, including information storage and retrieval systems, without permission in writing from the publisher, except by a reviewer who may quote brief passages in a review. For information contact the publisher at: McAndersPublishing@gmail.com.

Copyright © 2021

Get 6 FREE ebooks and an audiobook by signing up for Alex Anders' mailing list at: AlexAndersBooks.com
Official Website: www.AlexAndersBooks.com
YouTube Channel: Bisexual Real Talk
Podcast: www.SoundsEroticPodcast.com
Visit Alex Anders
at: Facebook.com/AlexAndersBooks & Instagram

Published by McAnders Publishing

Titles by Alex McAnders

MMF Bisexual Romance

Hurricane Laine; Book 2; Book 3; Book 4; Book 5; Book 6

*****

M/M Romance

Serious Trouble & Audiobook; Book 2

*****

Titles by A. Anders

MMF Bisexual Erotica

While My Family Sleeps; Book 2; Book 3; Book 4;
Book 1-4
Book 2
My Boyfriend's Twin; Book 2
My Boyfriend's Dominating Dad; Book 2

*****

MMF Bisexual Romance

Until Your Toes Curl: Prequels; Book 2; Book 3; Until Your Toes Curl
The Muse: Prequel; The Muse
Rules For Spanking
Island Candy: Prequel & Audiobook; Island Candy & Audiobook; Book 2; Book 2
In The Moonlight: Prequel; In The Moonlight & Audiobook
Aladdin's First Time; Her Two Wishes & Audiobook; Book 2 & Audiobook

Her Two Beasts
Her Red Hood
Her Best Bad Decision
Bittersweet: Prequel; Bittersweet
Before He Was Famous: Prequel; Before He Was Famous
Beauty and Two Beasts
Bane: Prequel & Audiobook; Bane & Audiobook
Bad Boys Finish Last
Aladdin's Jasmine
20 Sizzling MMF Bisexual Romances

*****

M/M Erotic Romance

Aladdin's First Time; Her Two Wishes & Audiobook; Book 2 & Audiobook
Baby Boy 1: Sacrificed; Book 2; Book 3; Book 4; Book 1-4

ASKING FOR TROUBLE

Chapter 1

Kendall

How many times have you put something into your mouth and thought, 'This does not taste good? Am I supposed to swallow it?' And then you do and you regret it. But seconds later you forget how much you hated it and put more of it in your mouth?

Well, that was me last night and I'm paying the price for it this morning. How can anyone drink whiskey? It tastes like dirt and it's like swallowing lava. I should have just held it in my mouth and spit it out when no one was looking. No one really cares if you swallow, right? They just care that you're there making the effort.

Okay, that's it for me. I know that it's a cliché for people to wake up with a hangover and claim that they will never drink again. But, I'm really not going to. I will never drink again. Not wine, not whiskey, not even a cider. I'm done with drinking. And, while I'm at it, I need to reconsider my relationship with loud noises and the sun.

"Can you quit that, please?" I said to my roommate Cory before groaning and rolling over feeling awful.

"I was putting on my pants," Cory replied confused.

"And, can you do it quietly?"

"How many ways are there to put on your pants?"

I groaned. "I don't feel well."

"Do you want me to get you a glass of water or something? I'm gonna go get breakfast. Do you want me to bring you back a bagel?"

I thought about a bagel with cream cheese and lox and almost threw up. What was Cory trying to do, kill me? Our dorm room wasn't very big, was he trying to get it all to himself? I moaned in reply and crawled into a ball.

Cory remained quiet for a moment and then sat on the edge of my bed and pushed his fingers through my hair scratching my scalp. It felt so good it almost made me forget that he had a girlfriend.

Aside from how loudly he put on pants, he was a very sweet guy. He was the type of guy I wished I could date if every gay guy didn't see me as quirky, and sexless, or their brother.

"I take it you had a good time last night?"

"I don't remember," I admitted.

"Did you black out?"

"Yeah," I told him burying my face in my pillow.

"Wow, that's rough," he said rubbing my head a little harder.

The man had magic hands. If I were a dog, my leg would be going wild right now. Girlfriend or not, if he wanted to crawl into bed and wrap his arms around me, I wouldn't have objected.

He wouldn't do that, though. Because besides being annoyingly straight, he was the purest guy I knew. No matter how innocent, he would probably think of it as cheating. The man was just a good guy. I would probably spend the rest of my life looking for a gay guy like him.

"Can I ask you a question?" Cory asked seriously.

"If I will marry you? If you're going to keep rubbing my head like that, the answer is yes."

Cory chuckled. "I'll keep that in mind, but that's not the question."

"Ooooh," I groaned disappointedly.

"I'm wondering why you have a piece of paper pinned to your shirt."

"What?"

Cory moved his magic fingers from my scalp and tugged at something hanging from my tee shirt. It was the one I was wearing when I headed out the night before. And until the moment my memories went dark, the pinned paper hadn't been there.

I rolled over to get a better look at it. Tilting it upwards, I saw words on it.

"It's written upside down," I told him as the whiskey's remains sloshed around in my brain.

Cory chuckled again. "Let me get that for you."

He released the safety pin and stared at the note. "Willow Pond @ 2pm. What does that mean?"

What did that mean? I knew Willow Pond. It was my favorite spot on campus. It was where I went when I needed a moment to think. But, what about "@ 2 pm"?

I was rolling over to ask Cory if he had read it correctly when an image suddenly flashed into my mind. It was of a boy of indistinguishable size and shape and he was leaning in to me.

"Oh god! I kissed a boy!" I said shooting upright.

Apparently, it was a little too quickly because with it came everything I consumed the night before. If our dorm room wasn't so close to the bathroom, I would never have made it. But when I returned from the porcelain god I felt like a tiger on the hunt. That lasted about 30 seconds before I was reminded that the sun was the devil and I had to crawl back under my sheets.

I wasn't exactly one of those popular gays who had a different guy in their bed every weekend. I would love to explain it by saying I was saving myself for marriage, but that wasn't it. Guys just weren't into me.

In high school, I could blame it on being the only out guy there. But, why was it the same in college? East

Tennessee University even had an LGBTQIA+ club. I was a member of it for my first two years here. Since during that time no one had asked me out, I decided to take a break from it this year.

What's a boy got to do to get some lip-on-lip action? Apparently, it's to get black out drunk where I can't remember what it felt like or who it was with. Great!

"Are you, okay?" My roommate asked looking at me concerned.

He was going to make some lush a great husband one day.

"I think I kissed a boy."

"I heard. Who?"

"I don't know."

"How could you not know?"

"Because unlike you, some of us make poor decisions and do things with complete strangers they don't remember," I explained.

"I make bad decisions sometimes."

"Sure you do, Mister I've-practically-been-married-since-I-was-seventeen. You probably don't even know what a bad decision is."

"I'm not perfect."

"Yeah, right."

"Whatever. So, do you think the guy you kissed is the same guy who wrote this?"

I sat up. "I do now."

"So, this is like an invitation?"

"To meet at 2 pm at my favorite spot?"

"Yeah," Cory said with building excitement. "That's kind of romantic."

"It is, isn't it?"

"Do you remember anything about the guy?" He said with way more interest than any straight guy should have.

I searched my memory. "All I can remember is someone leaning in to me. That's it."

"What about the angle? Leaning forward? Bending down?"

"He was bending down. And, he was big. I remember that."

"Big like actually big. Or just bigger than you."

"Hey, we're the same size," I reminded Cory.

"I wasn't making a judgment. I was trying to get a reference."

"I think he was big. Like, I think I remember him having large hands."

"Large hands," Cory said suggestively.

"What?" I said with a blush.

"I'm just sayin'."

Cory smiled. On top of everything else great about him, he was also the perfect gay best friend when I needed him to be. I knew it didn't mean anything and it was him being supportive. But, it did allow my fantasies to run wild every so often.

"Okay, Innuendo, hold your horses. We don't know anything about him. For all we know, he could be big because he was a statue my drunk ass was doing inappropriate things too."

"But, would a statue write a note telling you to meet him at Willow Pond at 2?"

I thought about that. Cory was right. Whoever wrote the note was human. The guy I kissed was made of flesh and blood. Did this mean that I had met someone I liked who liked me back? Were miracles real?

"Kelly and I are going hiking so I have to go grab breakfast. But you're meeting him, right?"

"You mean the stranger who could be arranging the place to murder me?"

"No, I mean the guy who kissed you under the stars and left you a trail to find him again."

Do you see what I mean about Cory being too good to be straight?

Cory got up and grabbed his keys and wallet.

"Kendall, as much as I've listened to you complain about not having anyone, there's no way you can't go. This could be the guy you spend the rest of your life with."

"Yeah, because he kills me and dumps my body in the pond."

Cory laughed. "Okay. Do what you need to do. But if I come back tonight and you haven't met this guy. I will be very disappointed in you."

"Yes, Dad."

"Good boy, son," he said before kneeling on my bed and kissing my hair.

Ugh! What did I say about Cory being perfect? There was no way that his girlfriend knew how great he was.

Enough about the guy leaving to meet his girlfriend and who I will never have. It was time to think about whoever it was that safety pinned the note to me. I had to admit that it was at least a little romantic.

Did he realize that I wouldn't remember the night and want to make sure that we would see each other again? That had to be it, right? Not that he didn't want to put his number in my phone for the police to find? Or, maybe it was both.

Slowly feeling my strength return, I searched my pocket for my phone. When I didn't find it, I searched my nightstand. It wasn't there either. Did I get so drunk I lost my phone?

Crap! It was $800 and I'm still paying for it. I am seriously never drinking again. It's a good thing that apart from my parents, the only other person on it was the guy I lived with. Thank god for being unpopular.

Needing to get something into my stomach, I eventually made my way to the cafeteria and filled my tray. I didn't know what would stay down so I got a little bit of everything. Looking up from my food, a guy I recognized from class caught my eye and waved me to join his group. I waved him off knowing I couldn't carry on a conversation in my state.

Besides, I wanted to see what I could remember before 2 pm. If I didn't know what he looked like, how was I going to find him when I got there? How did I know he wasn't staring at me right now?

I looked up and scanned the room. There were a lot of people. Most of them were engaged in conversation or staring down at their plate. The only one who wasn't was staring back at me. After a moment of eye contact, he came over.

"Hey Kendall, did you get my text about study group? Did you wanna join?" He asked awkwardly.

I knew him. It was the guy from psychology class who was always staring at me. I couldn't figure out what his deal was. Was there always something on my face or was he just looking at the guy behind me?

"I think I lost my phone," I said before wiping my mouth reflexively.

"Seriously? That sucks!"

"Tell me about it."

"Did you need my number again?"

"I don't have anything to put it in."

"Right," he said seeming disappointed. "Anyway, we're meeting on Thursday at Commons. It would be great if you could come."

"I think I have something on Thursday, but maybe," I told him not wanting to go.

"Oh, okay. Just let me know."

He smiled and returned to his table. I had to wonder about him. The guy was always asking me to join him for one thing or another. How many social events did he organize?

Finishing my pancakes, I felt human enough to return to my room and get ready for the day. Sunday was a quiet day at the dorms. Most people were usually shaking off the effects of their Saturday night.

Taking a shower I couldn't help but imagine who it was who had pinned the note to my shirt. What if Cory was right and it was the love of my life? The odds of it being him was low but it didn't mean it couldn't happen.

The thought of it made me tingle with excitement. What would it be like to crawl into a guy's arms and fall asleep? What would it be like to have a boyfriend or to have sex? I didn't know about any of that stuff.

All I knew was that no matter who this guy ended up being, I was going to do everything I could not to screw this up. I was tired of being alone. I wanted to know what love felt like.

With our meeting time approaching and the butterflies swarming in my stomach, I found the nicest tee-shirt I had and matched it to the same shade of black pants. Wrapping a studded leather bracelet around my wrist, I stood in front of the mirror and stared.

This guy was sure to be disappointed when he saw me in the light of day, but this was the best I could do. Brushing my unruly curls off of my forehead, they fell back. Yeah, this was as good as it was going to get for me. It would have to be enough.

Unable to put it off any longer, I left my room and headed to Willow Pond. I could barely breathe I was so nervous. What would happen if I couldn't recognize him? What if he saw me, realized he had made a huge mistake, and then left me standing there waiting.

The thought was almost enough to make me turn around, but I didn't. I continued step-by-step until the pond came into view. The place was practically empty. The only one there was a guy who stood along the shoreline staring at the ducks.

Could that be him? It couldn't be. I could only see his back, but from it, I could tell that he was way out of my league. Imagine shoulders broad enough to carry the world and arms strong enough to crush it in his hands.

His golden hair glistened as the reflection from the pond bounced off of it. The sight of him threatened to take my breath away. When he turned and our eyes met, it did. It was him, the guy from last night. I would have recognized him anywhere.

All of my memories came rushing back. Drunk off my ass, I had walked up to him at the party and had told him that he was the most gorgeous guy I had ever seen. I was expecting him to punch me or something. Instead, he asked me my name and we talked for the rest of the night.

Mostly I kept telling him how hot he was and tried to kiss him while he fought me off and blushed. Oh crap, I had forgotten about that. I had made a complete fool of myself.

He had only kissed me because I wouldn't leave him alone until he did. But then he wrote something on a piece of paper and told me that it was for tomorrow and that if I was still interested then, I should meet him here.

I think he had acted the way he had to be a gentleman. He had to have seen how drunk I was and didn't want to take advantage of me. But, how could someone be that hot and thoughtful? There was clearly something wrong with him.

"Kendall! You came," he said smiling through a rural Tennessee accent.

Oh God, he remembered my name. What was his?

"Of course," I said stepping within an arm's length of him. "How could I not…"

"You don't remember my name, do you?" He joked.

"I do. It's um…"

My thoughts tumbled desperately.

"That's okay. You were pretty drunk last night. I'm just glad you came."

"The note helped. It was pinned to me."

He laughed. "Yeah, I didn't want you to lose it… like your phone."

"So, I did lose my phone."

"That's what you told me."

"Crap! I was kind of hoping you had it."

"Why would I have it," he asked still smiling.

"I was just hoping. So, are you gonna make me ask you your name?"

"Oh. It's Nero."

"Kendall."

"I remember."

"Right. I have to be honest. I don't remember much from last night. The only things I do came to me about 60 seconds ago. Sorry."

"That's okay. What do you want to know? I remember everything."

I thought for a second. "Um, did we kiss?"

Nero laughed. "Yeah, we kissed."

"Was it good?"

"It was for me."

"And I was kissing you so it was probably good for me too."

Nero blushed.

"What did you tell me about yourself that I might have forgotten?"

"I don't think I told you much of anything."

"Why not?"

"You didn't ask. But I asked you a lot about yourself. I know that you're from Nashville."

"Born and raised," I confirmed.

"I know that you're a junior."

"True."

"And, I know that you're the cutest guy I've ever seen. But, you didn't have to tell me that."

My cheeks burned hearing his words. It clearly wasn't true, but to hear him say it sent a pulse through me that settled in my sex making me hard.

"You're pretty hot too," I told him knowing I was beet red.

"Thanks!"

"Since you know so much about me, I guess I should ask about you."

"Okay. Shoot."

"Where are you from?"

"It's a small town about two hours from here."

"And what year are you?"

"I'm a freshman. I took a few years off after high school."

"What's your major?"

"Right now? Football," he said with a laugh.

"Football?" I said feeling the air release from our bubble.

"Yeah. I'm here on a scholarship. So right now I'm eating and breathing it."

I stared at Nero not hearing another word after he said "football." A pain shot to the pit of my stomach until I was forced to cut him off.

"No! I'm sorry, no. I can't do this. Football? Hell no!" I said stepping away and pointing my finger. I stared at him again as the shock washed across his beautiful face. Why did he have to be a football player?

"Fuuuck!" I shouted in utter frustration before storming off and not looking back.

Chapter 2

Nero

What just happened? One minute I'm talking to the guy I had met the night before. Things were going well. I was feeling like he could be someone special. Then, out of nowhere he yelled at me and told me to fuck off.

"What the fuck just happened?" I shouted at Kendall as he walked away.

He didn't turn around or reply. A part of me wanted to chase him down and force him to tell me, but I wasn't going to. Did it have to do with me playing football? How? Why?

Football had always been what everyone liked about me. Even the people who hated me loved me when I stepped onto the field. Hell, even my mother loved me when I stepped onto the field.

For so many years she had been missing from my life. Not because she had abandoned me like my father. But because she had disappeared into her own world.

And the only time she would rejoin this one, would be cheering for me under Friday night lights.

Football had been how I and my newly discovered brother, Cage, bonded. Football is what is paying for my escape from the small town I grew up in. Football has given me everything good in my life.

But, the first guy I've ever admitted to liking, the first guy who has made my heart tumble just looking at him, hates me for having anything to do with it? Why can't I catch a fuckin' break?

Standing where Kendall had left me, my thoughts spun. It wasn't just that Kendall had walked off rejecting me. It was everything else going on in my life. Coming from Snow Tip Falls, big city life was hard. There was so much pressure. It took everything in me to stand out on the field. Waking up earlier than everyone else to run suicide sprints until I puked, was just the beginning.

Last night had been the first night I had felt okay about things. Meeting Kendall and him being so forward had made me think I could maybe be myself as well. I was as nice and considerate as I knew how to be with him. I really didn't want to screw things up. He was my chance to be who I really was for the first time in my life. And all of that had ended with him pointing his finger at me and yelling, "hell no."

That hurt. It ripped my guts out. I started walking so my head wouldn't explode.

Leaving the pond I headed to the street. It was the one that cut through campus. But instead of heading to my cramped dorm, I jogged in the opposite direction. I needed to get away. I needed to breathe.

My jog quickly turned into a run. As I did, my mind swirled. Thoughts of Kendall shifted to the last twenty-one years of my life. I had had to fight for everything. No one had given me anything. Not even my mother.

While she was catatonic, I went to work. Someone had to make sure we had a place to sleep and food to eat. By 14-years-old, the only person I could rely on was myself.

Most of the time I wore clothes that were a size too small. I couldn't afford anything else. And when the first kid at school pointed it out, I whooped his ass for bringing it up. No one made fun of me for it after that.

I went from doing errands that could have gotten me killed at fourteen, to betting on myself in fight clubs at 20. I had always done whatever it took to survive.

If Cage hadn't found me and told me we were brothers, I would probably still be doing it. Instead, he introduced me to his college football coach, arranged for my scholarship, and rescued me from that world.

Yet even with how far I've come, the guy I fell for still thinks I'm too hard to love. That had to be why my mother chose to vanish into her own world and why I grew up without a father. I was too hard to love. I was a nobody worth nothing and that was all I was ever going to be.

Thinking that, everything became too much. My head throbbed and a painful agony ripped through me. I felt like I was going to explode. I needed to release it. So, doing it the only way I knew how, I locked my eyes on the next parked car in front of me and let go.

Kicking the door as hard as I could, the metal bent on impact. It wasn't enough. I needed to hear a crash. So balling my fist, I pounded on the passenger window. It wouldn't give in so I slammed harder. Eventually, the glass exploded into a thousand pieces.

As loud as it was, that still wasn't enough. Kicking the back door I dented that. About to climb on the hood and put my foot through the windshield, something stopped me. It was a siren. It woke me up as if I had been lost in a bad dream.

Clearing my head, I stared at what I had done. I had demolished the car. This was bad. I had lost control of myself and this was the result.

"Get on the ground!" Someone yelled behind me. "I said get on the ground."

I had just ruined everything. I was about to lose my scholarship and my only shot at life. If I were a smarter person, maybe I would have run. I didn't have it in me.

I had done this. I had been the one to mess up everything good that I had going on, no one else. And I wasn't going to fight my self-inflicted destruction.

Not getting onto my knees fast enough, someone shoved me from behind. I fell landing on the broken glass. Before I could get off it, someone was pulling my wrists together and slapping on cuffs. They were tight enough to cut into my skin.

"You have the right to remain silent," he began.

I didn't have to listen to the rest. I was familiar with it. I was going to jail. Since I couldn't afford bail, they were going to hold me for two to three days until I went up before the judge.

From there I would be sentenced. And unlike when I was under aged, this crime would follow me for the rest of my life. I had done this to myself. And to be honest, I always knew it was a matter of time before I screwed things up.

I followed the cops' instructions without resistance. In the back seat of the squad car, I let my mind wander. I thought about all of the things that had gotten me here. I thought about Kendall. Of all of my regrets, the fact that I had made him so upset was at the top of it.

The truth was that last night's party wasn't the first time I had seen him. It was the day of Cage's graduation. We had locked eyes as he stood under a tree watching the ceremony. I thought he was the cutest guy I had ever seen.

He wasn't a big guy, but dressed in all black, he had a bit of an edge to him. His shaggy brown hair highlighted his angular features. And completing his I-don't-give-a-fuck look with delicate, round-rimmed glasses told me that there was more to him than he let on.

There was more to me than I let on. I was the thug who hosted fight clubs for money. I was ready to take someone out at the drop of a hat. But, I liked guys. All I ever wanted was for a guy to hold me in his arms and tell me that everything was going to be alright.

When I saw Kendall standing there, I desperately wanted to do that for him. Maybe no one would ever do that for me, but I could be his rescuer. I wanted to protect him. I wanted to give Kendall the love I could never have. But the moment I was given an opening, I fucked things up by being myself.

At the station, I answered all of their questions and was escorted to my cell. There were two other people there. One looked drunk off his ass, and the other… well, he looked like me, a thug whose time had run out.

I wasn't in the mood for talking and neither were they. This wasn't my first time in jail so knowing I would be there for a while, I got comfortable. It was to my surprise when a cop appeared on the other side of the bars and said my name.

"Nero Roman?"

"That's me."

"You made bail. Let's go."

I got up sure he had made a mistake. But if they were going to let me out on a filing error, I was okay with that. Walking back to the sea of desks, I scanned the room spotting someone I didn't expect to see. Quin was my brother's boyfriend and he was looking pretty freaked out.

Considering Quin's parents had more money than God and he grew up vacationing in places like the Bahamas, no wonder being in a police station made him look like he was about to pee himself. The only question was what he was doing here. I hadn't used my one phone call. I couldn't think of anyone who would help me.

When I got within arm's length, Quin threw his arms around me. His embrace was genuine and tight.

"Jesus, Nero, what happened? What are you doing here? And, why didn't you call me?"

I was about to answer when someone else I knew walked through the doors. Titus was my roommate and a guy I knew from back home. He had been inspired to attend East Tennessee University by the same two people I had, Quin and my brother. He approached and threw his arms around me too.

"What the hell is going on, man? And why did we have to hear you were here from some guy at campus security?"

"It's nothing," I told them. "I just did a little damage to a car."

"A little damage?" Quin asked pulling away. "They said you smashed in a window and a couple of doors?"

"Like I said, a little damage," I said with the hint of a smile.

"Why?" Quin begged, his cutely nerdy face narrowing.

I thought about Kendall and how he had told me to go to hell.

"I don't wanna talk about it. You guy's got a ride out of here?"

"Yeah, I'm driving," Titus told me pushing his fingers through his shaggy, coffee-colored hair. "I'm parked out front. Let's go."

The three of us headed to Titus's truck and drove back to campus in silence.

"Where am I headed?" Titus asked as we turned onto Campus Lane. "Am I dropping everyone off or are we headed to Quin's place for our usual Sunday dinner?"

I was about to ask him to take me to our dorm when Quin cut me off.

"My place. Cage is driving down and he's going to want to hear about all of this. It may as well be over food."

"You didn't tell Cage, did you?" I asked Quin feeling a pain in my chest about it.

"He was the first person I called after Titus told me."

I looked at Titus pissed.

"Look man, Campus security told me you had destroyed one of their cars and was in jail. Who else was I supposed to call? He was the only one who would know how to get you a lawyer."

"You called a lawyer?" I asked Quin.

"I didn't have to. Cage called the school and was able to smooth things out. He still has a lot of good will from winning them those national championships. So, all I had to do was put up your bail and get you out."

"So, I'm not gonna lose my scholarship?"

"I didn't say that. But, I'm sure Cage will tell you everything you need to know about it. Seriously, Nero, what were you thinking?"

I didn't reply.

"So we're headed to Quin's place?"

I looked out the window resigned. "Yeah."

"Cool. Lou told me he didn't have a date tonight, he's gonna be there too," Titus said with a smile.

Both Quin and I looked at him.

"What? He and I are friends. I know neither of you has much experience with having friends, but trust me, hanging out is a thing people do."

I turned to Quin. We were both thinking the same thing. Titus never talked about it, but living with him, I was definitely getting the sense that we had more in common than either of us was admitting.

Titus and Quin's gay roommate were pretty close. I knew that being friends with a gay guy didn't mean anything. And Titus was a very friendly dude. But, I couldn't help but think how cute the two of them were together.

I would never say that to Titus because I wasn't ready for the guy I lived with to see that side of me. It was one thing to let little things slip in front of my brother's boyfriend who had a lot of practice keeping secrets. It was another to tell the person who saw you every day and watched your comings and goings. That was too much pressure considering I had barely figured things out. And after what happened with Kendall, I realized I knew even less than I thought I did.

Parking in front of Quin's fancy dorm room, we headed up and were greeted by Lou.

"You brought the criminal," he said staring at me. "What did it end up being? Armed robbery? A B&E?"

"How do you know what a B&E is?" Titus asked.

"I watch Law and Order. I know things."

Quin interjected. "I don't think Nero wants to talk about it. So..."

"It was a classic smash and grab wasn't it? Look, don't think because you have this whole bad boy thing going on you're going to get me to fall in love with you. I like nice guys."

I opened my mouth to reply.

"Okay fine, we can go out. But if you get me pregnant after a drunken night of lovemaking, I'm having the baby and I'm not raising him alone."

I looked at Lou stunned and then laughed. We all did.

"I'm serious, Mister. I'm not raising Nero Jr. by myself."

"Okay, I promise," I told him suddenly feeling better about things.

Titus spoke up. "Now that we got that settled, how does everyone feel about a game of Wavelength?"

Wavelength was our go-to Sunday night game. Mostly it was over drinks and when things were a lot less tense.

Pairing up, Titus grabbed Lou, of course, and I partnered with Quin. Playing a couple of rounds, things were good. Then Cage arrived.

My brother was pissed. I couldn't blame him.

"Why the hell did you smash up a campus security car?"

"It was a campus security car?" I asked.

"You didn't know?"

"It wasn't like I was targeting anybody. I was just mad."

"About what?"

"Nothin'," I said really not wanting to talk about it.

"Don't want to say, huh? Well, you're gonna have to talk about it. The school's willing to let you pay for it instead of pressing charges."

"I don't have the money."

"You're the one who destroyed it. You're going to be the one to pay for it."

"I could lend you it," Quin volunteered.

"I don't need your money," I snapped.

"Watch it, Nero. He's just trying to help."

"I don't need his help. I don't need anyone's help."

"Considering he was the one who bailed you out of jail, that doesn't quite seem true, does it?"

I shut up knowing Cage was right. As soon as I stopped talking, so did Cage. With a lot more sympathy in his eyes, he approached me and put his arms around my shoulder.

"Nero, you have a temper and you're gonna have to get control of it."

"I'm trying."

"And yet, my boyfriend had to bail you out of jail today."

"I don't know what to say," I admitted.

Cage stared at me. I guess he didn't know what to say either.

"I'll think of something. I'll talk to the school and see what we can come up with. Don't worry, we'll get this straightened out. I'm here for you, man. I'm not going anywhere."

"None of us are," Titus added.

"Yeah," Quin agreed.

I looked at the guys around me and wiped a tear from my eyes. Maybe everything would be alright. Maybe I wasn't as alone as I thought.

Chapter 3

Kendall

"Ahhhh!" I screamed popping awake.

I looked around. I'm in my bed and it's morning. Cory is sitting up staring at me. He looks startled.

'It was just a dream,' I tell myself. 'That's all it was.'

"Evan Carter?" Cory asks me slowly relaxing.

"Evan Carter," I admit.

"Fuckin' Evan Carter," my roommate said making me feel a little better.

I lay back down and tried to calm myself. I couldn't tell if the nightmares were getting worse but they weren't getting better.

Evan Carter was the football player who made my high school years hell starting my freshman year. There was something about me he couldn't stand. I always assumed it was because I was the only out gay kid there. But if I were honest with myself, it wasn't like I tried to fit in.

I experimented with the color of my hair, wearing makeup, and the type of clothing I wore. Perhaps wearing a dress to school was a little too far. It wasn't like I was fighting to bring down the patriarchy or anything. I was just having a little fun. I was trying to figure out who I was.

FYI, I'm not a guy who wears dresses or makeup. And it isn't because Evan Carter would bully me to an inch of my life when I did. It just isn't my thing.

But, there had to be some point when the football meatheads couldn't take anymore. Because from a certain point forward, they would shove me every time they passed me in the hallways. I could be eating lunch or sitting quietly in class and my head would jerk forward followed by the sting from their open palm.

They would shove my head into desks, locker doors, and even toilets. The worst part was I could never see them coming. It got to the point where my entire school day would be spent searching rooms for them. When I spotted one, I had to make myself as invisible as possible. If they saw me, they could attack or not. It was always random. But when they decided that today was my hell day, I wasn't safe anywhere.

And, if it wasn't the physical abuse, it was the constant teasing. I know there's nothing wrong with the word 'sissy' and a lot of guys wear it as a badge of honor. But, if I hear it one more time, I think I'm gonna crack.

I wouldn't give in, though. I refused to let their closed-mindedness control my life. I would cry as I got dressed in the morning knowing that what I was putting on would bring about another hell day.

I got to the point where I didn't even want to wear it. But I did it anyway because… who knows why anymore?

Maybe it was to prove to myself that I wouldn't succumb to pressure. Maybe I didn't want to give them the satisfaction of thinking they had won. Maybe I was just a glutton for punishment.

Whatever the reason, I did it and I barely had the will to live by the time high school was done. I was so glad to start university and get past all of that. I could dress how I wanted, and I could be my true self. I thought it was the greatest thing ever until the nightmares started.

Granted, they were always there. But now they sharpened and focused around one person, Evan Carter. He was the leader of the bunch.

I still believe that if it wasn't for that idiot, the rest of them would have left me alone. He was probably a closet case who wished he had the courage to do what I had. Who knows?

But, what I'm sure of is that, in high school, I lost the battles and the war. Not only was I the only one getting his ass kicked on a regular basis, he owned real estate in my head years later. It was such bullshit.

The really sucky part was that until last night, the nightmares seemed like they were beginning to fade. I used to have them up to a couple of times a week. Cory knows all about that. The number of times I had woken him up screaming, it's a wonder he's still willing to be my roommate.

It had been two weeks since my screaming fest before last night. I'm pretty sure I know what triggered it. I had kissed a football player. The thought almost made me throw up. Sure, Nero was nothing like Evan Carter or any of his asshole friends, but still.

Football players have made my life a hellish nightmare of epic proportions since I was 14-years-old. They threatened my will to live. I wake up screaming and dripping in sweat because of them. I didn't want to suck on a football player's face now.

"You going to class?" Cory asked me not having left his bed.

"Oh fuck!" I exclaimed remembering my early Monday morning class.

My professor had to be a sadist. Who scheduled a core class at 8 am on a Monday? It's ridiculous. But, if I wanted to become a clinical psychologist, I needed to major in psychology and I had to take it.

I scrambled out of bed and quickly got dressed. Getting ready, I loaded my backpack and hurried out. I walked into class late but tardiness was graded on a curve at 8 am.

"Today you will be filling out the T.E.Q., The Toronto Empathy Questionnaire. Not only will it lead us into our discussion on empathy, it will tell you wannabe therapists out there whether you are right for the job," my professor said suddenly grabbing my attention.

I very much wanted to be a therapist. It was the only thing I had wanted since I was 12. I had read a Psychology 101 textbook cover-to-cover when I was 15-years-old because I was so interested in it. I needed to do well on this test.

When the paper was slipped in front of me, I saw that it wasn't very long. The questions were also fairly basic. I put my name on it and began.

'When someone is excited, I tend to be excited too; never, sometimes, or always?'

Easy. Always, of course.

'Other people's misfortunes do not disturb me a great deal; never, sometimes, or always?'

Again, easy. Never... usually.

I mean, if it were a normal person, who I assume this question is referring to, I never feel good about someone else's misfortune. But, let's say Evan Carter gets hit by a bus. I'm not suggesting that he die... necessarily. I'm just talking about him feeling a fraction of the pain he put me through for four years.

The question can't be referring to situations like that, could it? Or, did it? Was the questionnaire trying to dig out your darkest thoughts? Was my lack of empathy for a psychopath who tortured me what will make me a bad therapist?

I stared at the question paralyzed. I couldn't get past it. I couldn't believe that after everything he put me through, the echo of it could prevent me from being good at the only thing I had ever wanted.

"Please hand your papers forward," my professor said snapping me out of my trance.

"I'm not done," I told the grabby girl who took my paper from me and passed the stack along.

She shrugged barely acknowledging my struggle. I knew for sure that that ice queen would make a horrible therapist. But what about me? Was empathy really that important?

I didn't have to wait long to get an answer to that question. Two days later, my professor asked me to see him before I left.

"At the beginning of the semester I asked you all what your goals were for the class," Professor Nandan began.

"Yes. And I said that I wanted to become a therapist, because I do."

He looked at me confused. "Right. Which makes me wonder why you would do this on a questionnaire designed to determine your level of empathy," he said before placing my sheet on the desk between us.

"I know, I didn't finish it."

"You didn't. But that's not what I'm talking about," he said placing his finger next to the doodle I had drawn in the top right corner of the paper.

Looking at it again, I realized that it was less of a doodle and more of a sketch. I was known to draw on things when I was bored, and they weren't always happy pictures. This one was decidedly not happy and had a message that was hard to miss.

"You drew a football player hanging from a noose in the corner of an empathy questionnaire? Is there something you would like to talk about, Mr. Seers?"

My mouth dropped open as I looked up at the rounded-faced man in front of me. There was no question what had inspired this. Fuckin' Evan Carter.

"Okay, I can explain," I began not knowing what I would say next.

"Go on," he urged patiently.

Was I going to lie? Tell him the truth? This was feeling like a no-win scenario.

"I might have an issue with football players."

"You don't say," he said sarcastically.

"And, I might have woken up from a bad dream about one of them right before coming to class."

"Did you want to talk about that dream?"

"Not really. It was a pretty standard nightmare. Lots of chasing. Lots of running. You know, the usual."

"And then you came here and drew this... on an empathy questionnaire?"

"It would seem," I said with an uncomfortable smile.

Professor Nandan leaned back in his chair and stared at me. I couldn't tell what he was thinking but I couldn't imagine it was anything good.

"The way we deal with childhood trauma is unique to each of us," he began. "Some of us choose to avoid it. But the most effective strategy for having a healthy, happy life is to deal with issues head-on."

"You're suggesting I should see a therapist about it?"

"It wouldn't hurt. But, what the research shows is that the most effective way to gain empathy for a group is to humanize them."

"I don't think football players aren't human. They're just the worst ones who ever existed."

My professor looked at me strangely.

"Right. But you do accept that not everyone who shares a trait is the same? Not every football player is alike. Just like how not every student who dresses in all black and studded bracelets are alike. We are all unique individuals."

"What are you suggesting?" I asked feeling a knot tighten in my chest.

"I'm suggesting you get to know a football player. I think if you see their individuality, it might go a long way to helping whatever negative feelings you have towards them. It might even help your dreams."

"And, how do you suppose I get to know a football player?"

"Interestingly enough, there is a program I've been trying to put together for a few years. It's kind of a mentorship thing. Upper-class students are matched with freshmen who are having a hard time adjusting to university life to act as someone they can lean on. Considering your goal is to become a therapist, this might be up your alley."

"That sounds great. But, I'm guessing what you're not saying is that I would be mentoring a football player."

"There's one that has gotten into a little hot water for his behavior. And instead of expelling him from school and the football program, the university thought that something like this would be helpful."

I stared at my professor. Worst idea ever! Not the whole thing. The mentorship part sounded pretty cool. But the part about me being locked in a room with one of those pig-throwing psychopaths was insanity.

Was he looking to get me killed? As soon as the door was closed and we were alone, this guy would dislocate his jaw and swallow me whole. Having devoured me, he would most likely slither his way to Washington D.C. growing in size until, with his tail wrapped around the Washington Monument, he would eat the president turning the United States into a demonic dictatorship… or was I overreacting?

"Yes," I said before it registered in my brain. "I'll do it."

"You will?"

"Apparently."

"Are you sure?"

"No. But, yes. Look, I want to be a good therapist someday. Hell, I don't just wanna be good. I wanna be great. I wanna help people. I want kids to not have to go through what I did growing up. And if that means confronting my issue with a certain group of demonic soul suckers, I will."

Professor Nandan looked at me questioningly.

"I'm kidding… mostly. No, I'm kidding. I can do this. And you're right. Confronting my issue head-on is the best way to handle this."

"Then I'll set it up. Thank you for this. If this works out with you and him, it could lead to a lot of people receiving help for years to come," he said with a smile.

"In other words, no pressure?"

He laughed. "No pressure. Just be you. It's not about you being able to provide him with any answers. It's about being there for him and lending him your ear when he needs it."

"I could do that."

"You'll do great," he said before promising to email me the details and sending me off.

It was a good thing that no one actually needed sleep to maintain their sanity. If they did, I would have been in a whole lot of trouble. Because lying in bed in the dark, all I could think about was everything Evan Carter and his teammates did to me since I was old enough to pee straight.

I didn't know what I was thinking when I agreed to do this. Me mentoring a football player was a bad idea, a very bad idea.

That wouldn't stop me from going through with it, though. Who was I to reject a bad idea?

Walking to the agreed-upon meeting spot, I was sweating through my clothes. I was having a full-on panic attack. We were meeting in the serpent's den, the football team's practice facility. But at least my professor was going to be there with me.

"You ready for this?" He asked me as excitedly as I was terrified.

"No, but I'm here. So, let's do it."

Professor Nandan put his arm around my shoulder and led me into the room. The beast sat with his back to me. The funny thing was that I recognized his back. It was unmistakable. And when he turned around and I got a glimpse of his to-die-for cheekbones, I thought this was a cruel joke.

"You?" I asked stunned.

"Do you two know each other?" My professor asked.

We stared at one another. I didn't know how to respond.

"We've met," Nero replied.

"I'm hoping that's good," my professor suggested.

Nero looked at me again. "Yeah," he confirmed allowing my professor to breathe.

"Then perhaps I don't need to introduce you two. But, Nero Roman, this is Kendall Seers. Kendall, Nero is a very promising football star."

"I don't know about all of that," Nero quickly interjected.

"I've seen you play. You're very good," the older man gushed.

"Thanks," Nero said looking away bashfully.

"And Kendall, here, is one of my most promising students."

"I am," I confirmed. "Probably his best."

I have no idea why I said that. But it broke the tension. At least for those two.

"I don't know about all of that," my professor joked. "But he's very good. You should be in good hands with him. Should I leave you two to get to know each other?"

"I don't see why not," Nero said looking at me like I hadn't spit in his face and kicked dirt on him as I walked away the last time I saw him.

"Very good. Then I'm off," the glowing man said before leaving us alone and closing the door behind him.

We both stared at each other. It would have been the worst thing in the world if he wasn't so goddamn hot. Seriously, how could someone be that good-looking? The guy oozed sex. I considered what he looked like naked.

"So, what do you wanna talk about?" He asked me smiling. God did he have a great smile.

I thought I was sweating before. Now I was practically standing in a puddle.

"Are you hot in here?" I asked. "I mean IT! Is IT hot in here? Do you want to get out of here? Let's get out of here. I need some fresh air. I can't breathe in here."

"Are you okay," he asked concerned.

"I just need to take a walk. Can we take a walk?"

"Whatever you want," he said dripping with small-town southern charm.

We left the practice facility and walked back to campus in silence. Halfway there I realized I wasn't going to be able to walk away from this, so I headed to a bench and sat down. Nero sat next to me. I could smell him. He smelled like leather and musk. The scent made my dick hard. What was I doing getting hard for a football player?

"How did you know?"

"How did I know what?" I asked still not looking at him.

"That this was my favorite spot. I don't remember telling you that the night we met."

"This is your favorite spot?" I asked finally turning towards him.

"Yeah. I stop here every day after practice. Practice is always a lot, you know. Everything can be a lot. So this is the bench I sit on to get my thoughts right."

I looked around. I hadn't spent much time on this corner of the campus during my years here. But it was a beautiful spot. There were more trees here than any other part. And with the colored fall leaves blanketing the ground, the scene looked like a postcard.

"What is it that gets to be a lot?" I asked suddenly feeling calmer.

Nero's smile disappeared. "You name it. Practice. Classes. Having feelings I probably shouldn't have."

I stared at Nero wondering what those feelings were. "Can I ask you something?"

"What's that?"

"Are you gay?"

Nero shifted uncomfortably. I don't think he was prepared for the question.

"You don't have to tell me if you don't want to."

"It's not that I don't wanna tell you."

"It's that you don't know?"

"Is that bad?"

"What does "good" or "bad" mean?"

"Well, one is something that's good. And the other is something that's bad," he explained with a serious look.

I turned to him. He dropped the seriousness and we both laughed.

"Oh, that explains it. I never saw it in that way before," I joked.

"You're welcome," he said playing along.

"I meant, what is a moment of uncertainty in the grand scheme of things."

"It's been longer than a moment. It's been since puberty if we're gonna put a date on it."

"And, who did you have feelings for before that?"

"Mostly girls."

"Then, you're probably bisexual," I told him.

"But, I've had very strong feelings for guys. Especially recently."

"It doesn't matter. Bisexuality is defined as the ability to have a romantic or sexual attraction to more than one gender, not necessarily at the same time or in the same amount. So, if you had a genuine crush on a girl when you were 12, and I mean strong feelings, then you've proven that your brain is wired in such a way that you can have those feelings. There's no need for you to have another crush to qualify it."

"Then I would guess that would make me bisexual. Wow! I've wondered about that my whole life and you just answered it for me," he said amazed. "So, what about you?"

"What about me, what?"

"Are you bisexual?" He asked shyly.

"Oh god no! Do I look like an animal?"

Nero stared at me shocked. I let my statement hang out there as long as I could and then laughed.

"I'm kidding. Not about being bisexual. I'm gay. But, I would be fine with it if I was."

Nero relaxed and laughed. "Hey, maybe you are bi. Maybe you just haven't met the right girl yet."

"Yeah, that girl better come with a dick because that's pretty essential to my fantasies."

"That could happen," Nero pointed out.

"True. But still, there's something about a guy that draws me to them. It's hard to explain…"

"No, I get it. There's something about them," Nero said looking at me and making me hard again. God was he sexy.

"Anyhow, enough about my non-existent love life. Maybe you could tell me what landed you here."

"Here?"

"You know, having to hang out with me."

"Luck?"

I laughed. "I'm serious."

"Me too," he said with a bucket of charm.

"No, come on. I'm supposed to be here to help you. My professor said that you had an incident?"

Nero looked down and dropped the charm.

"Yeah, I had a run-in with a car."

"What do you mean?"

Nero hesitated and looked at me.

"Sometimes things can get away from me. When they do, I don't always make the best decisions."

"So, when you say you had a run-in with a car...?"

"I might have taken out some frustration on it."

"Oh!"

"I dented a couple of the doors, smashed a window..."

"Why?"

Nero stared at me for a moment and then looked away.

"I don't know. There are just times when things get away from me."

"Have you always been like this?"

"Probably."

For all of his charm, there was no mistaking what I saw. He wasn't a monster. He was a guy in a lot of pain. My heart broke for him.

"Things can get away from me too, sometimes."

"Yeah?" He said looking back at me.

"Yeah. Like when I said what I said to you."

"Oh."

Nero looked down. There was no mistaking the pain that memory triggered.

"I know you will never guess this, but I have a thing against football players."

Nero smiled. "I might have picked up on that. Why?"

As comfortable as I was starting to feel around him, I wasn't yet ready to go there.

"How about we not talk about me?"

"Then what should we talk about?"

"What's going well for you right now?"

"So far, today's going pretty well," he said finding his charm.

"Come on."

"It is. And, I guess you can say football's going well."

"What does that mean? Have you been catching a lot of passes, or something?"

"Yeah, I play running back which means it's my job to catch passes and run down the field. I've been doing it a lot."

"Sounds great," I said mustering as much enthusiasm as I could.

"You have no idea what that means, do you?"

"No, I do. Catching… Passing… The field is that big green thing with the stripes, right?"

Nero laughed. He had a nice laugh.

"Yes. That's the field. I have an idea. You want to get to know me, right?"

"For professional purposes," I made clear not wanting to lead him on.

He tried to hide his disappointment. It shouldn't have, but him being disappointed about that gave me a charge.

"Right, for professional purposes. Then you should come watch a game."

All of my fears about football players came rushing back.

"I don't know."

"You should. I can get you tickets. You can bring someone, maybe your boyfriend?" Nero asked hesitantly.

"Wasn't my drunk ass trying to kiss you a couple of nights ago?"

"I remember something like that," he said feeling good about himself.

"Then what makes you think I would have a boyfriend?"

"I don't know. Maybe you have an open relationship or something. Guys do that sometimes, don't they?"

"This guy doesn't," I said firmly.

"Good. Neither do I. I mean, not that it matters…"

"Not that it matters," I confirmed.

"So, will you go? I could seat you next to my brother and his boyfriend?"

"Your brother has a boyfriend?" I asked surprised.

"Yeah. He's pretty cool, too."

"Who? Your brother or his boyfriend?"

"Both, actually. And my brother used to play football here so he could explain everything you need to know about the game."

"So, your brother is an ex-football player who has a boyfriend."

"We football players come in all types," Nero said with a smile.

"I guess," I said still trying to wrap my mind around that.

"So, are you coming?"

I thought about it for a second. Before I could decide, I heard myself say, "Yes". My mouth had a mind of its own lately.

"That's awesome!" He said with delight.

His excitement was genuine. I liked bringing him joy. It felt good to know I had. So, although I wasn't sure about it, I was gonna go watch a football game. Who was I becoming? What would spending time with Nero turn me into?

Chapter 4

Nero

If I knew that smashing up a car would get me to spend time with a guy like Kendall, I would have a long time ago. Staring into his eyes did something to me. All I could think about was kissing him. I wanted to slide my fingers into the hair behind his ear, pull him to me, and press my lips on his.

"Hey, did you end up finding your phone?"

"No. I had to get a new one."

"That sucks!"

"Yeah."

"I'll have to give you my number so you have something to put in it."

Kendall looked at me with a suspicious smile.

"I can text you the details of Saturday's game."

He stared at me adorably and then gave in.

"Sure."

Standing in front of him exchanging numbers, I thought about all of the things I could do to him instead of saying goodbye. I didn't do any of them. Staring at him, my heart raced. I felt alive when I was with him. It was like the weight of my past was lifted.

Deciding to wrap my arms around him and never let him go, he stuck out his hand.

"It was good meeting you… again," he told me professionally.

"Oh. Yeah. It was good seeing you," I told him before shaking his hand and walking away still tingling from talking to him.

After a few steps, I couldn't help but look back so I peeked over my shoulder. I caught his gaze. He was looking back, too. A rush of heat washed through me. When he quickly turned around, I did the same.

He clearly wanted to keep things professional. I could respect that, though I definitely didn't want to. I wanted to do things to him that I barely dreamed of doing with another guy.

Before seeing Kendall at Cage's graduation, my feelings for guys had been different. I imagined us spending time together and me holding onto them as we slept. Maybe we would go skinny dipping, or maybe we would get naked and he would give me a massage after a hard game.

But, I wanted to kiss Kendall. I wanted to strip him down and push my hand over his naked flesh. I wanted his dick in my mouth. I wanted to taste his cum. I wanted to roll him over and remove all the distance that separated us by pushing my cock into his tight ass. I wanted to hear the noises he would make as I entered him.

Thinking about it, I immediately became hard. It happened a lot when I thought about Kendall. I didn't know how I was going to keep my head in Saturday's game knowing he was going to be there.

One thing for sure was that I needed to have the best game of my life. I needed Kendall to see me on that field and realize that he didn't want to keep things professional. Once he did, I was going to pull him into my arms and everything would be perfect.

Heading back to my room to relieve myself of the tension that had built up, I entered and was surprised to find it full of people.

"Cage, Quin, what are you doing here?"

The two looked over at Titus.

"I'll give you three some space," Titus said quickly heading for the door.

Still feeling charged from my time with Kendall, I had to hide the bulge stretching across the front of my pants.

"Hey bro, do you have a second to talk?"

"Yeah, what's up," I agreed getting nervous. "You guys aren't about to tell me you're breaking up, are you?"

Both of them looked at me shocked.

"God no. Things have never been better between us. Why would you go there?"

"I don't know. Things have been going so well lately that I figured something would screw things up."

"Things have been going well? Didn't you smash up a car less than a week ago?"

"Yeah, but things have gotten better."

"That's good," Cage told me before looking over at his silent boyfriend.

"So, things have been going well with us, too. In fact, Quin and I were thinking about taking things to the next level. We'd like to move in together."

I thought about what he said. The only reason I was able to attend school was that after graduation, he moved to Snow Tip Falls and was looking after our mother. For the last eight years that had been my job. But Cage, who was working as the football coach for the local high school, was living with her in our mobile home. It was the arrangement that made my new life possible.

I looked at Quin. "You wanna move into the mobile home?"

"Not exactly," Quin said looking at Cage to explain.

"Quin was thinking about buying a house in Snow Tip Falls. That way he doesn't have to stay in Dr. Sonya's bed and breakfast when he comes for the weekend."

"So, you want to move out of our place? Who's gonna take care of Mama? Are you expecting me to come back and do it?" I asked feeling a clench in my chest.

I was enjoying my new life, especially now that Kendall was in it. I wasn't ready to give it all up.

"No. That's not what we're trying to tell you," Cage explained. "We're telling you that Quin is thinking about buying a house where we could all live. Mama would have a room. You would, too."

"I could even get something with four bedrooms so that we could have somewhere for guests to sleep when they visit. I'm sure my parents would want to visit at some point. We're going to need enough space for them too."

"So, you're just gonna buy a four-bedroom house so you two have somewhere to hook up every other weekend? Must be nice."

I didn't mean to be a prick to Quin about how rich he was. But as a guy who had to do some fuckin' awful things to survive over the years, it was a tough pill to swallow.

"Don't be an asshole, Nero. He's offering us somewhere to live rent-free. Aren't you tired of living in a place with no privacy? I mean, how did you even have girls over when you were growing up? The walls are paper thin."

"I didn't have girls over," I told him not mentioning the main reason I hadn't.

As much as I was into girls, the feelings I had had for boys had always messed with my head enough to force me to keep my distance from them. I'm sure I could have been with one if I wanted. There were plenty of girls who made that clear. And the fact that I didn't act on any of those opportunities just added to my anger.

I couldn't get myself to be with girls. I couldn't get myself to be with guys. My mother was lost in her own world. I didn't see a way I would ever be loved. That really fucked me up.

"Well, if you have a bedroom with a real door, maybe you could."

I looked over at Quin. He clearly hadn't mentioned the hints I had been dropping about my feelings towards guys. I knew that Quin had picked up on them. The guy was literally a genius.

The way I understand it, his parents did some sort of procedure to artificially conceive him and it made him one of the smartest people in the world. So, figuring out my closeted ass had to be like reading a pop-up book for him.

"You guys coming to my game on Saturday?"

Cage flinched at my change of topic.

"Of course."

"The person they assigned me for that anger management program they put me in is gonna be there too. He doesn't know much about football. Do you think you could, you know, explain things to him? I just don't want him to be bored to death. I want him to have a good time."

"No worries. We got you. How's the program going, by the way?"

"I was a little nervous about it. But, it might work out?" I said thinking of Kendall.

"You seem happier," Cage pointed out.

After he said that I realized I was smiling. "Maybe."

"We'll make sure he has a good time," Cage agreed. "What's his name?"

"Kendall."

As soon as I said it I felt my cheeks heat up. They stared at me like my feelings for him were written on my face.

"Okay, yeah. We got you," Cage said with a smile.

"Don't worry about a thing," Quin said telling me that Kendall would be in good hands.

Texting Kendall about his ticket, he replied with a simple, 'Thank you.' I was hoping for a little more. If he was still into me, wouldn't he have at least wished me luck on the game?

I remembered what he said to me the night of the party. Drunk-Kendall had made clear that he wanted me.

The same was true when we met up on Sunday before he found out I played football.

But, maybe that was no longer true. That motivated me even more to have the game of my life. I had to win him over. The only thing anyone ever liked about me was what I did on that field. I was going to get Kendall to like me.

Thinking I would be distracted entering the stadium for the game, I was wrong. I had never been more focused in my life. Titus, who was a bench warmer on the team, tried to talk to me. When I ignored him, he got the message and made sure I had my space.

Staring as our defensive team started the game, everything slowed down. I could see where everyone would move before they got there. So, when I took the field with the offense, I looked into the quarterback's eyes. Immediately he understood.

Chapter 5

Kendall

Entering the stadium had to be the most out-of-body experience of my life. I was walking into the lion's den willingly. I couldn't tell you if I was doing it for professional purposes. Or if I was doing it because I would get to see the guy I was crushing on again.

Neither changed how shaky I felt crossing the halls looking for my seat. Everything about the place triggered me. I seriously didn't want to be here. I would have turned around and walked out, if it wasn't for the hot guy I had come to see.

Did I say "hot"? I meant the "troubled" guy who needed my help. I needed to remember what I was to him. I might not be his official therapist, but he needed to know that he could trust me. I couldn't cross that line.

Remembering that, I pushed aside my hesitation and pulled myself together. Finding my section, I waded into the sea of seats. This was not like my high school stadium. It was huge. It had to seat 20,000 people. It was overwhelming. All I wanted to do was find my seat and pretend I was someplace else.

"Are you Kendall?" a friendly guy said in an east coast accent as I sat down.

I looked at him and then the hulking guy beside him. The big guy had to be Nero's brother. They didn't look that much alike, but they were both the hottest guys I could imagine.

The guy who had greeted me was good-looking too, but he would better be described as cute. He was about my size with the same hairless face. I wouldn't exactly describe him as nerdy. But, he was definitely someone I wouldn't expect to be at a football game.

"I'm him. And you're…" I pointed at him and blanked on his name.

"Quin. This is my boyfriend, Cage."

"Nero's brother?"

"That's me," he said with the most charming smile. Did killer smiles run in their family?

"Nero told us to make sure you have a good time," Quin told me welcomingly.

"Did he?"

"He definitely did. So, have you ever been to an East Tennessee game before?"

"I've never been to any type of game before."

"Oh. Neither had I until I met Cage. They're fun. You just have to get into the spirit of it."

"I'm not much for team spirit," I explained.

"It helps to have someone to cheer for," he said turning to the field. "Okay. We're East Tennessee so we're in blue. That's us over there. And, Nero is…" Quin searched the field for him. When he mentioned Nero's name, my heart skipped a beat. I swallowed. "There he is," he said with a smile.

I turned and found him. He was one of the guys going to the center of the field.

"Do you know the premise of the game?"

"I know nothing," I told Quin.

"Simply put, they're trying to get the ball through the end zone which is past that line there. So, here you go, they are setting up a play and…"

Quin stopped talking when someone handed the ball to Nero. With it, a guy from the other team dove towards him. Nero spun shaking the guy off of him and then sprinted towards the end zone.

The other team chased him. Each time Nero would dance around them or spin by them. The crowd stood as he got close to the line. I stood with them. And when Nero dove into the air to escape the last person attacking him, he crossed the line. The crowd exploded. I didn't care about football, but not even I could escape being swept away as 20,000 people roared.

"Does that always happen?" I asked leaning over to Quin.

"No, it never does. He ran 90 yards for a touchdown on the first play."

"I guess he has his head in the game," Nero's brother confirmed. "I wonder what inspired that?" He said looking at Quin. Both of them then turned to me. I knew what they were implying, but I wasn't going to acknowledge it.

At the same time, the thought that I had anything to do with what Nero had just done, sent my body awash in tingles.

"Everyone says that Nero is really good," I said prodding them for more.

His brother replied looking proud. "It's early in the season but so far he leads the division in yards run."

"That's good?" I asked Quin hoping for a translation.

"He's doing it as a freshman which means that he might have a shot at going pro."

"That's if he can keep his head on straight," Cage added. "You're supposed to be helping him with that, aren't you? How's that going?"

They both looked at me.

"He ran 90 yards on the first play of the game. You tell me," I said suddenly caring whether they wanted Nero and me to be together.

Cage laughed. "Yeah, maybe you'll be good for him. Nero could use a few more good things in his life."

I didn't know what that meant, but I made a mental note to find out.

I had to admit that watching the game wasn't as terrible as I thought it would be. As I understood it, Nero scored three more touchdowns, which was very good. And Quin turned out to be someone I could really relate to. He was a great guy. Both of my hosts were.

I couldn't get myself to warm up to an ex-football player entirely. But the fact that he was with someone like Quin, who had to have gone through what I had in high school, made me think that he wasn't all bad. Maybe not every football player was a complete jerk.

"We're going to meet up with Nero and grab something to eat. Would you like to join us?" Quin asked.

I hesitated. There was no question that I wanted to see Nero. If nothing else, I wanted to congratulate him on the game. But, wouldn't the professional thing be for me to go? I didn't want to make Nero think that something could happen between us. As good as that was starting to sound, it couldn't.

"Join us," Quin insisted. "I'm sure he would love to see you."

"Okay," I said without thinking.

"Great!" Quin said with a smile.

"So, you're from Tennessee?" Quin asked as we made our way through the stadium.

"Nashville. And you?"

"New York."

"Oh wow! What was that like?"

Quin exchanged a knowing look with Cage. "Unique."

"How so?"

Quin then explained his complicated childhood. The guy had two fathers and a mother, and grew up as rich as God. He mentioned something else about going to a small high school for gifted kids and I was officially obsessed with him. Not in the way I was obsessed with Nero. But, obsessed. I wanted him in my life.

Our conversation only stopped when Nero exited one of the hallways and joined us. Another guy followed him. As soon as Nero spotted me, our eyes locked. I felt hot staring at him. Every part of me wanted to kiss him again.

"You made it."

"Of course."

"I'm glad. I hope these two didn't bore you," Nero said pointing at Quin and his brother.

"No. I wouldn't have understood what was going on without them."

"I'm Titus," the friendly guy behind Nero said offering me his hand.

"I'm Kendall."

"And, how do you know our star, here?"

"I'm, umm," I looked at Nero not sure what I should say.

"He's a friend," he said staring into my eyes again.

The silence drew out.

"Okaaaay," Titus said grabbing everyone's attention. "Is anyone else starved? Riding the pine can build up quite the appetite."

I looked at him confused and then turned to Quin. "Riding the pine?"

"It's what they call it when you're on the team but you don't get to play in the game."

"Oh."

"Yep. Not everyone gets to play as a freshman like ol' Nero, here. Then again, not everyone can play like him either." Titus grabbed Nero's shoulders and shook him.

Nero lowered his head and blushed. I would never have guessed Nero was humble.

"So, is Lou joining us?" Titus asked the group.

Quin replied. "No. He has a date."

"Huh," Titus said looking a little disappointed.

I looked at Quin.

"Lou's my roommate."

Something told me that there was more to the story than that. I wasn't about to ask.

As the group walked to a nearby pizza place, Nero fell back and walked with me.

"How did you like the game?" He asked me with a proud smile.

"You were impressive. I could see why everyone says you're so good."

"It was my best game of the season. I finally felt like I had something to play for."

"Yeah, Quin told me that you have a chance at going pro."

Nero laughed. "Yeah, that's what I mean."

I guess that wasn't what he meant. And guessing what he actually meant made me hard.

"Did Cage and Quin make you feel comfortable?"

"They did. Quin's really cool. He's like a regular guy."

"If you think he's a regular guy, then you two didn't talk enough," he said with a laugh.

"No. Right. He's about as far from regular as you can get. I meant that he's gay and he doesn't make a big deal about it."

"Make a big deal?"

"You know, some guys can make a whole show about it."

"Oh, you mean Lou?" Nero joked.

"Oh really?"

"Yeah. He's a show. You don't like that?"

"I don't know. I guess it's more that, I'm over it. I think I used to be a bit of a show."

"You?"

"Yeah. I hadn't figured out who I was."

"You didn't know if you were gay?"

"Oh, I knew. Everyone knew. I just didn't know what type of gay. And not everyone appreciated my discovery process."

"Does that have something to do with how you feel about football players?"

I looked at Nero knowing that I had kept my feelings on them vague.

"It has something to do with it."

"Well, I hope you're beginning to see that we aren't all like that."

"I'm starting to," I said with a smile.

"So, what you're saying is "Thank you, Nero, for opening my eyes. For, they were closed before and now you have changed my life forever"."

I laughed. "I don't know about all that."

"That's okay, you can say it. You don't have to be embarrassed. You're among friends."

I gave him a playful side-eye and left him to talk with Quin. I really did like Quin and he seemed to like me too. Although this was my third year here, the closest thing I had to a friend was Cory, my roommate. He was great but also very straight. Quin was not. That made a difference.

At the pizza place, I sat next to Quin and continued talking to him. Every so often I would look up at Nero and catch him staring back. Each time I caught him, it gave me a rush. He was kind of an amazing guy. I was starting to see that. But that didn't change that it was my job to help him, not get into his pants.

Though, talking about getting into his pants, when we were walking to the pizza place, I had glanced down below his belt. The bulge that stretched across the front of him was impressive. It was almost enough to make me forget everything, strip him naked, and ride him like a bull. Almost.

When the bill came, Quin grabbed it and no one made a gesture to pay. I offered to pay my share but he brushed me aside.

"You can get the next one," he told me. "Hopefully we can hang out again."

"Yeah, definitely."

I wasn't sure if he was talking about the whole group or just the two of us. Either way, I wanted to. I wouldn't have guessed that meeting Nero's friends would have gotten me to like him more, but it did. It was getting harder for me to keep things professional with him. And when he said bye to everyone else and walked me back to my room, it took everything to remember that this hadn't been a date.

"Did you have fun today?" He asked with the sexiest bashful smile.

"I did. Your friends are pretty cool."

"They liked you. And, I think you made a love connection with Quin."

I laughed. "Yeah, too bad he's taken."

Nero smiled. "I guess you'll have to settle for whoever's left."

"Bummer," I said teasingly.

"Bummer."

Staring into his eyes I recognized this moment. I might not have had any experience with guys or relationships, but I knew that if this was a date, this would be the moment he bent down and kissed me. I wanted him to. But as soon as he leaned towards me, I stepped away and offered him my hand.

"Anyway, thanks for giving me a glimpse into your world. It was…"

"Life-changing?" Nero asked quickly shaking off whatever disappointment my gesture created.

"Yes, life-changing," I conceded. If I wasn't going to kiss him, the least I could do was make him feel good about himself.

"Thought so," he said cockily. He stretched out his arms. "Hug?"

I hesitated, but only for a moment. Slipping my arms around him, I held him tightly. When he did the same, I didn't want him to let me go. Even after he loosened his grip, it took me a moment to reciprocate. I was falling for Nero and I was falling hard. The only question remaining was what I was going to do about it.

Chapter 6

Nero

From the moment I released Kendall from my arms, I couldn't stop thinking about him. I had played out of my mind knowing he was watching me and that intensity followed me into my next practice.

"Keep up the hard work, Roman," Coach said as I puked in a bucket after wind sprints.

"Thanks, Coach."

Getting his acknowledgment felt good, but not as good as receiving one of Kendall's texts. I was trying not to text him too much. I didn't have much experience with this but my gut told me I should play it cool. But what the hell did I know other than it was crazy that I was choosing to go through this alone.

A year ago, my brother had gone through the exact thing after meeting Quin. I wasn't sure why I hadn't come out to him yet. It wasn't like he was going to judge me for it. Besides, after the display I put on when we got pizza, there was no way he didn't know I was head-over-heels for Kendall.

'Could you drive Quin to Snow Tip Falls this weekend? We have a house we want you to take a look at,' Cage texted.

I stared at the text not sure how to respond. I was happy to drive Quin up and it would give me an excuse to see Mama. That wasn't the problem. It was the part about the house.

Their plan made sense. There was no use in Quin paying to stay at Dr. Sonya's bed and breakfast if he could buy something as easily. And, lord knows it would be good to have a little privacy when I came to visit. You couldn't fart in the old place without everyone knowing about it.

But, as run down as it was, the old place was home. It was mine. Actually, it wasn't. We paid too much to rent the shit hole. But — I don't know — it was my home. It was somewhere no one could take from me — except the landlord who had threatened to kick us out a lot over the years.

I didn't know why I gave a shit about that crap hole at all. But, I did. And the thought of losing it made me feel uneasy.

It's not that I didn't trust Quin's hospitality. Hell, at this point, Quin felt as much like family as Cage did. There was no way those two weren't getting married. Everyone knew that.

I just didn't know if I was ready to be dependent on someone else. I had had to take care of myself for a long time. When you only have yourself to rely on, there's only one person who could let you down.

Sitting on my bed in my dorm, the door opened.

"Hey, Cage said he texted you. Did you get it?" Titus asked before tossing his backpack to the foot of his bed.

"I got it. I've been busy. I haven't gotten the chance to reply."

I could feel Titus staring at me as I stared at the ceiling lost in thought.

"I can see that. Genius at work," he joked. "Did you hear that Dr. Sonya's organizing a festival?"

"A festival?"

"Yeah. The Moonshine Festival. Cage is helping. Dr. Sonya thinks it can bring in tourists. Considering the town's history of running moonshine, I think it's a good idea. And if there's anything people are willing to drive for, it's alcohol, right?"

"Maybe."

"I don't know. I think it'll work."

I watched Titus as he grabbed a cup of noodles and heated it in the microwave. "So, what's up with you and Lou?"

"What do you mean?" He asked casually.

"I mean, do you like him or…"

"Of course I like him. We're friends."

"That's not what I mean. What I'm saying is that you two spend a lot of time together. Is there a reason for that?"

Titus turned to me as if caught in a lie.

"What reason do you need more than we're friends? He's a fun guy. I don't have to tell you that."

"I guess not."

"So, what's the deal with you and Kendall?"

I looked at Titus not having expected the question. It was clear why he had asked it, though. Titus was there on Sunday. It wasn't like I was hiding the way I felt about Kendall.

"We're friends and he's a fun guy. You've met him. I don't have to tell you that."

Titus stared at me and then barked a laugh. He knew what I was saying. If he wasn't going to be truthful with me about the way he felt about Lou, why should I share my feelings for Kendall?

"Right," Titus conceded. "Don't forget to text your brother back," he reminded me before collecting his soup and leaving the room.

I took out my phone and typed, 'Sure.'

'Great. I'll see you then,' he immediately replied.

I still wasn't sure about them getting a house, but I started to realize that there were other things I had to talk to him about. I had already put it off too long.

Driving up after I got back from my away game, Quin and I arrived in Snow Tip Falls past 8 pm.

"Are you coming by our place or should I drop you at Dr. Sonya's?"

"Cage said we should meet at your place. I wanted to say hi to your mom. We'll head to Dr. Sonya's later."

I paused remembering something. "By the way, have you made any progress on that thing you were looking into?"

"You mean about who your and Cage's father is?"

"Yeah."

Cage had been kidnapped from the hospital as a baby and had spent his life living with the guy who snatched him thinking his mother had died in childbirth. But then Cage met Quin. In a few weeks, Quin had figured out, that the man who raised him wasn't Cage's biological father, which hospital Cage was born in, and had found us.

Quin was able to figure out the two of us were brothers based on nothing. The guy was super smart. And, since my mother never told me who my father is, who, it turns out, is also Cage's father, I asked Quin to look into it. I knew he had been working on it, but he hadn't given me an update in a while.

"What I've learned is that it probably isn't anyone in town."

"Seriously?"

"Yeah. Why? Did you suspect someone?"

"I thought so."

"Well, I could be wrong. But I've been talking to your mother about it. She's been doing a lot better lately. And she certainly isn't willing to say much, but she gave me the impression that she moved to town after she got pregnant with you. I'm thinking that if it was someone in Snow Tip Falls, she would have been living here before she got pregnant with Cage."

"So, you're not basing it on any of your science-y stuff?"

"I can't just ask every guy in town to take a paternity test."

"Not every guy… And, you didn't need a test to know I was Cage's brother."

"That's different. You guys have the same rare genetic traits. Besides, I've been keeping my eyes open for that. So far your mother is the only one I've found who has them."

"So, again it's down to getting my mother to spill the beans and she's not talking."

"I'm afraid she's not. And, maybe that's a good thing."

"Why would my growing up not knowing who my dad is be a good thing? At least Cage had that guy. He might have been a piece of shit for doing what he did, but he was there. Mama was all I had. When she lost her marbles, I had no one. How could that be better?"

Quin stayed quiet for a while before answering.

"Nero, I think there's something going on that you might not want to know about. After talking to your mother, I'm starting to think that it might be better left in the past."

"What do you mean? Do you know something you aren't sayin'?"

"No. I've told you everything I know. But, have you ever wondered what set your mother on her downward spiral?"

"Yeah. Of course. It was when Cage was snatched, and the hospital lied and said that he had died. She knew it wasn't true."

"That's what she says and that's possible. But, you said she didn't get bad until you were much older. So, how was she able to hold it together for so long? And, what finally sent her over the edge?"

"It wasn't, like, one thing. It was gradual. I watched it."

"Yeah, but maybe you weren't watching what you thought you were. Maybe there was something else going on."

"So, you're saying something triggered her checking out on things?"

"That's my guess. And, my other guess is that, whatever it is, you may not want to know."

I thought about that for a while.

"You tell Cage any of this?"

"Cage hasn't asked about it."

"So, you're only gonna bring it up if he asks?"

"Probably."

"Which is why I had to ask you about it?"

"Yeah," Quin said with a serious look on his face.

"Don't you think Cage would wanna know this?"

"Maybe. Maybe not. He's found you and a mother after living his life without a family. For him, that's enough, at least for now."

"Are you sayin' that finding Cage and having a brother should be enough for me?"

"I'm not suggesting anything. But, I'll ask you, isn't your life pretty good right now?"

"It's not bad," I admitted.

"Then, why would you want to kick the hornet's nest?"

I looked at Quin and fell into silence. The guy was smart and had made some good points. But growing up as he did with two dads, he couldn't imagine what it was like growing up without one.

He meant well with his advice. But to answer his question, sometimes you kick the hornet's nest because it's in the way of you living your life.

It was clear that Quin wasn't going any further with his investigation. That left me where I was when I started. My mother was still the only person who had the answers and she wasn't talking. What was she hiding? And could it be something I didn't want to know?

I continued to think about it as we entered town and headed towards the trailer park. The closer we got, the more my thoughts shifted to the other thing I had to talk about this weekend. My jaw clenched as it whipped through my mind. I didn't know if I was ready to discuss this, but Cage and Quin's lives were moving forward. It was time that mine did too.

Pulling up to my place, I saw Cage's truck parked out front. Going inside, we found him and Mama on the couch in front of the TV. When she didn't turn around to look, I stared at my mother.

What was she keeping from me? What could be so bad about my birth? And after a lifetime of asking, how could I get her to tell me now?

"Dinner's ready if you're hungry," Cage said turning to greet his boyfriend with a kiss.

Sitting around the kitchen table, for the first time I realized how small it was. With four people, the plates could barely fit at the same time. As the smallest person, Quin was tucked in the corner. There was no wonder he was willing to buy a house. Dealing with all of this had to be a nightmare for him.

"When are you planning on showing me the place?" I asked Cage.

Cage looked at Quin and Mama. That was when I realized that he might not have told our mother yet.

"It's a nice house," Mama said to my surprise.

"Oh! So, I'm the only one who hasn't seen it?"

"You haven't been around," Cage explained.

"That's because I have games on Saturday and classes during the week."

"We know. We're not saying anything about it. Just, that's why you haven't seen it."

I looked at the three people in front of me. Everyone's lives were moving forward. And, they were doing it without me.

"So, when am I gonna see it?"

"Tomorrow morning. Miss Roberts said she can open it up at 9."

"Why so early? It's a Sunday. Don't you people sleep in anymore?"

"She said she has to be at the Salon by 10 for appointments."

"People get their hair done on a Sunday?" I asked having lived here my whole life and never realizing it.

"Church. Bingo. Get-togethers. It makes sense," Cage explained.

"I guess."

I looked at the three people I cared most about wondering if this was the time. It wasn't. I was going to let Cage and Quin show me their house first. That was the better plan.

After Cage and Quin took care of the dishes, they headed off to Quin's bed and breakfast. I joined Mama on the couch. Her mental state had been night and day since Cage had entered our lives. It made me wonder if her life would have been better if I was the one who had been snatched instead of my perfect older brother.

"You good, Mama?" I asked putting my hand on hers.

"I've been feeling good, son. In fact, I've been meaning to tell you, I've been thinking about looking for a job."

Her words stunned me speechless. Seven years ago, it was her unwillingness to hold a job that made me have to support us. I was a kid doing things that no kid should have to do.

Now she was telling me that she was ready to get back to work? What the hell was going on?

"What inspired this, Mama?"

"I've been feeling better. Having Cage back has made all of the difference in the world. Don't you love having your brother back?"

"I do. He's good for you, Mama."

"He's good for all of us."

"Yeah, he is," I said wondering if her improvement also had to do with her secret.

One thing became clear as I lay awake that night. No matter what had sent her spiraling years ago or what had brought her back, my Mama no longer needed me. No one did. I could probably take off tomorrow without them noticing I was gone. That was a tough pill to swallow, but it was true.

Despite how tired my body was from the hits I had taken during Saturday's game, I didn't fall asleep until after 4 am. That meant that I wasn't awake by 9:00. It was a phone call at 9:15 that woke me. I didn't need to ask why Cage was calling. So, I just picked it up and said,

"I'm leaving now. Where am I going?"

"I texted you the address."

I looked at my screen. "Got it. Be there in 10."

I recognized the address. Being a small town, there weren't many really nice neighborhoods. The house I was headed to was in one of them. The house closest to it was owned by Glenn, who owned the local general store, and his husband Dr. Tom, the town's only doctor. That meant that Quin's house had to be nice.

Pulling up to it, I turned out to be right. The place was two-story with a huge veranda and an equally large yard. The ceiling of the veranda was shiny cedar. As were the floors in the giant kitchen and dining room.

Actually, there were two dining rooms, as well as two living rooms, even though Quin called one a family room. There was also a three-car garage.

On top of that, there was marble and chandeliers everywhere. The bathroom attached to the master bedroom had a claw-foot tub in it. And where there weren't the nicest hardwood floors I had ever seen, there was brand new carpet.

This had to be the most incredible house I had ever been in. I had thought Dr. Tom's house was fancy, but there was no comparison. This place had to cost half a million dollars. The rent for our mobile home was $300 a month.

"You can just buy this place?" I asked Quin.

"I mean, my parents will help me out with the down payment. But, I've been working for my father this semester."

"While taking classes?"

"Yeah. And, the investments I've identified for the company have paid off. I'm lucky."

"Must be nice," I told him still floored by what I was seeing.

"Yeah, Nero, nice for us, because we're the ones who are going to get to live here," Cage said giving me a look as he grabbed Quin and kissed his head.

"Yeah," I said half-heartedly. "Listen, there's something I've been meaning to talk to you guys about."

Cage let go of his boyfriend and both moved in front of me.

"What's up?" Cage asked.

"So, you guys know that I've been playing well."

"We know. Your game last Saturday was insane."

"Yeah. Yesterday wasn't that good, but it was close," I informed them.

"That's fantastic. I'm proud of you, bro."

"Yeah, me too," Quin said enthusiastically.

"Thanks. But, you know how after someone has a few good games, people start talking about you going pro?"

Cage chuckled. "I remember it well."

"That's started happening to me."

"Yeah?"

"Yeah. And, I'm considering it."

"You mean this year?" Cage asked surprised.

"Why not? I'll be 21 by draft time. That's the same age as most people going into the draft."

Cage looked at me concerned.

"You get that running backs aren't what NFL teams are looking for right now, right? If you get an injury, you could fall far."

"I get all of that. But the iron's hot now. I may as well use it."

"That's true," Cage said not as excited for me as I hoped he would be.

"And, I get that you had the chance to go #1 in the draft but chose us instead…"

"Hey, I didn't go pro because I was injured."

"You don't have to bullshit me. I know you were feeling better in time to make it. And even if it wasn't last year's draft, you could have made it this year."

"But I didn't want that."

"Yeah, you wanted to be with us."

"I did."

"And now I'm choosing to go pro instead of doing what you did," I said lowering my head.

Cage put his arm around me and squeezed my shoulder.

"Nero, I made the decision that was best for me. I needed this. What's more, I wanted this. But because I chose this for myself doesn't mean you have to.

"The world is big. You should explore it. I can hold down the fort. I'm here so you don't have to be," Cage said with a smile. "You hear me?"

I felt a tear on my cheek that I quickly wiped away.

"I hear you."

"Good."

Cage let me go and rejoined Quin. I watched them get comfortable in each other's arms.

"There's probably something else I should tell you now that we're talking about stuff."

"What's that?" My brother asked.

"I, ah, I think I want what you have?"

Cage twisted his head confused. "What I have?"

"You know, Quin," I said vulnerably.

"Bro, Quin's taken," he said with a smile.

"You know what I mean."

"Actually, I don't."

"Come on," I said not wanting to explain myself.

"You need to say the words," Cage told me no longer hiding what he knew.

My chest hurt looking at the two caring faces staring back. Taking a deep breath, I gathered myself. This was it. I was going to say it out loud.

"I like guys. I think I've always liked guys. I might like girls too, but it doesn't feel the same with them. It never has. And, it's possible I've found a guy I really like."

"Kendall?" Cage offered.

"Yeah. Was it that obvious?"

"I wouldn't call it obvi…"

"Yes," Quin said cutting him off. "We could all see it. And, I like him. He could be good for you."

"You think so?" I asked looking for encouragement.

"Yes. He has a way about him. He's very empathetic."

"He wasn't very empathetic when he found out I was a football player."

"What happened?" Quin asked stepping out of Cage's arms.

"He basically told me to go fuck myself. I mean, he didn't use those words, but he may as well have."

"That surprises me. Did he say why?"

"I asked him and he wouldn't talk about it."

"Maybe you should ask him again," Cage suggested.

"Some people need a little encouragement to talk about things," Quin added.

Cage looked at Quin. "Says the guy with no filter."

"Yes. There were things about me that I wouldn't have told you if it wasn't for Lou."

"So, I owe all of my happiness to Lou?"

"I'm hoping I can take a little credit for it, too," Quin said with a smile.

"Baby, I give you credit for making my life everything I've ever dreamed of. I can honestly say that I wouldn't be the man I am or have anything I do without you."

"Ohhh!" Quin said tilting his head back and kissing his love. "Let's take the house. I want to live here with you, Cage Rucker."

Cage looked up at me. "What do you say? Should we take the house?"

I looked at the couple I wanted to be. "You should take it," I said with a heavy heart.

I knew I shouldn't think this way, but it felt like the end of everything I had loved. Things were changing. There was no space left for me. I had to make things work with Kendall. If I didn't, I was going to be left with nothing.

Miss Roberts, the realtor, was as excited as Cage and Quin were that they were going to take the place. She promised to draw up the paperwork saying that we would be able to move in in about a week. Quin thought it was fast. I had no clue about these things.

Deciding to spend the day with them, I tagged along when they headed back to Dr. Sonya's bed and breakfast. I had only been there once before and I hadn't passed the doorway. This place was very nice as well. It was starting to feel like everyone had more than I did. It wasn't the first time I had thought that. But seeing how other people lived, it had never been clearer.

"Oh good, you brought help," Dr. Sonya said with her usual high energy. "I was needing a few extra hands and here you are," she said squeezing my arms in delight.

Dr. Sonya put us all to work. Her son walked downstairs, saw us, and immediately headed to the door.

"How are you getting out of helping?" I asked recognizing him from high school.

Cali was a freshman when I was a senior. He was also second string on the football team. I remembered him not being much for talking. That hadn't seemed to change.

Ignoring my question he said, "You just started at East Tennessee, right?"

"Yeah. You thinking about going?"

He looked back at Quin.

"I was thinking about it."

"You're a senior, right?"

"Yeah."

"You still a kicker?"

"He made a 60-yard field goal in a game last week," Cage said proudly.

"Jesus! That's insane. You could be a walk-on as a freshman with a foot like that."

"He could get a D1 scholarship with a foot like that," Cage confirmed. "East Tennessee would be lucky to get him."

Cali turned red as we talked.

"Well if you need me to put in a word with the coach, let me know," I told him.

"Mr. Rucker said he would take care of it for me."

"Mr. Rucker?" I asked confused.

"Me," Cage said annoyed.

I laughed. "Right! Mr. Rucker. Well, I'm sure you're in good hands. He got me my scholarship."

"And now they're lucky they have you. Don't screw things up. I need my credibility in tack for this one," Cage joked.

"Oh shit! You're screwed," I said turning to Cali.

Cali looked at Cage scared.

"He's kidding. Nero, tell him you're kidding."

"I'm kidding… sort of."

Cali looked at me not sure what to think.

"Cali, do I hear you in there?"

Cali looked towards the kitchen then quickly slipped out the door. Dr. Sonya entered the room and looked around.

"You just missed him," I told her. "He mentioned something about football." It was technically true.

Dr. Sonya looked at Cage. Cage shrugged.

"Well, he left more fun for us," she concluded with a smile.

For the most part, the doctor had us making signs. They were on large placards and required a lot of filling in. After we were all high on the marker fumes, she fed us and let us escape her festival organizing clutches.

Free, the three of us did a hike. There wasn't a lot to do in Snow Tip Falls, but the hiking trails were world-class. The town got its name from what the waterfalls looked like in the winter. The rest of the time, the hikes were just a tree-lined miracle of nature. It was worth the trip.

As Cage and Quin chatted, I thought about what was going on between me and Kendall. I would love to invite him up and show him all of this. He seemed more like a city boy, but so was Quin before coming here. Now, he hiked through the woods like he grew up here — As soon as I thought it, Quin tripped on a root and got a face full of dirt.

"You okay?" I asked knowing he was.

"Yeah, I'm fine. I just didn't see the root."

"That's because you're too busy talking," I said teasing him. "It's a hike, not a chat-a-thon."

"Chill out, Nero," Cage said defending his man.

I could respect that. Because I did, I let it go. But, the two of them did a fair bit less talking after that.

I didn't actually mind their endless chatting. The only thing that got to me was that I didn't have Kendall here to do the same. Thinking of him again, I pulled out my phone to see if he had texted.

"Checking for a message from Kendall?" Cage asked teasingly.

"Chill out, Cage," I told him.

Not finding one, I stuffed my phone back in my pocket. After a moment of silence, Cage spoke again. This time with more empathy.

"He'll text. I saw the way he was looking at you after the game. He's into you, too."

"I said chill out, Cage!"

Despite my reaction, I appreciated what he said. Every time Kendall took an extended time to reply, I wondered if things between us were over. He had already told me to go to hell once. Should I expect him to do it again?

I had to figure out the thing he had against football players. He was helping me deal with my shit. As a football player, maybe there was something I could do to help him.

Not returning to Dr. Sonya's labor camp with my siblings, I headed home and waited for Cage to deliver Quin. Driving back, Quin and I talked about Kendall. He suggested that we invite him to our next game night. It wasn't a bad idea. But I felt like I needed alone time with him before we did.

'When are we doing our next session?' I texted him when he didn't reply to what I thought was a funny meme.

'If you want, we can talk over lunch tomorrow.'

'What about over dinner at Commons?' I asked referring to the cafeteria connected to the popular study space. It was a little more intimate.

After our rapid-fire exchange, Kendall didn't respond for an hour. When he did, he wrote, 'Sure. What time?'

I couldn't have been happier. Seeing him was all I thought about for the rest of the night.

Going extra hard in practice to burn off my excess energy, I was exhausted by the time dinner rolled around. I could barely lift my arms.

"What's up with you?" Kendall asked me after looking me up and down.

"Hard practice."

"Oh. So, what have you been up to?"

I wanted to say that he would have known if he had replied to my text, but I didn't.

"I took Quin home on Saturday. He and Cage wanted to show me the house they're buying together."

"They're buying a house? How is it?"

"It's the nicest house I've ever been in."

"Really? Wow."

"I could show you at some point. The realtor said they could move in in a week."

"Oh. Yeah," Kendall said unenthusiastically.

"Okay. I gotta know. What is it that you have against football players?"

"I don't have anything against them!"

"Says the guy who told me to eat shit and die as soon as I mentioned that I was one."

"I didn't tell you to eat shit and die."

"You may as well have. I could tell that was what you were thinking."

Kendall didn't reply.

"If this is gonna work, you know, whatever it is that we're doing here, you're gonna have to let me in a little as well. I can't be the only one spilling my guts out."

"That's not the way therapy works," Kendall insisted.

"Well, this ain't therapy. If that's what this was, I wouldn't have agreed to do it," I said meaning it.

I could tell he knew I was being serious. He was slow to reply.

98

"Fair enough. I guess I have a small chip on my shoulder when it comes to football players."

"Small?"

"Okay, fine. I have a giant boulder. I have the Grand Canyon on my shoulder. You happy?"

"Actually, no. Why do you have such a big problem with them?" I asked a little heartbroken.

"Because they made my life hell. To this day I still wake up drowning in sweat after dreaming about what happened to me."

"What happened to you?"

"Just a lot of little things. Walking in the halls, they would push me or knock my books out of my hand. They would say things about me liking guys. They would de-pants me?"

"They would pull down your pants?"

"Yeah. A lot. And I never knew when it would happen. I could be walking to class or talking to someone and one of them would grab my pants and there it went. They didn't even care what they pulled down. Once I was in the doorway about to enter class and someone yanked everything down. I ended up standing there with my dick out.

"I mean, not too many people saw, but it was still humiliating, you know? So, yeah, I have a problem with football players. Get it now?"

Listening to Kendall tell me what happened, my face got so hot it felt like it was on fire. I was blackout-mad. The rage that bubbled in me was beyond anything I thought I could control, yet I had to have looked as calm as hell because he asked me if I had heard him.

"I heard you. Would you like an apology?"

"You don't have to apologize," Kendall said looking down.

"Not from me. From them."

"I'm not gonna get an apology from them."

"I didn't ask if you were gonna get one. I asked if you wanted one," I said as prickles rippled under my skin.

"I mean, I guess."

"Then, let's get you one."

"What?"

"Do you know where any of them live?"

"I mean, I know where all of them live. I wouldn't be able to sleep at night if I didn't."

I closed my eyes absorbing what he said. He couldn't sleep at night if he didn't know where they were. That was insane. There was no way in hell I was going to let them get away with doing that to him. There was no way.

"Then we're going," I got up trying to be as calm as I could.

Kendall didn't move. I looked back at him.

"I can't tell if you're serious or not. I mean, you look serious, deadly serious. But…" He looked at me again. "You know it's a three-hour drive to Nashville, right?"

"Two hours and forty-five minutes. I know," I told him.

"Wait, how do you know that?"

"Kendall, are you coming with me or not? Because one way or another, I'm gonna get you that apology. But I would prefer you be there to hear it."

"I don't know."

"Kendall, I'm not asking you. I'm telling you. Let's go."

As soon as I said it, a smile crept across his face. "Okay," he agreed. Then, without another word, he followed me to my truck and we were off.

Navigating to the highway, neither of us spoke. Broiling, I didn't want to speak. I felt like I did when I was driving to one of my fights at the club. I would let everything that had pissed me off in life float to the surface and I would sit with it. By the time I arrived, I would be ready to rip people's heads off. That's what I felt now.

"Where?" I asked Kendall when the highway offered an off-ramp.

"Stay on 40," he replied until we approached the Nashville city limits. "Get off here," he said directing me onto 155 and then into a neighborhood called Porter Heights.

Kendall's eyes bounced from house to house. It was a nice neighborhood. There were a lot of two-story brick homes on large properties. It had long ago become dark so I couldn't tell much else about the place, but I was ready for whatever was going to happen next.

"What's his name?" I asked Kendall who was now crackling with anticipation.

"Evan Carter," he said scanning every home as we slowly drove around. "There! Park there."

We pulled up in front of one of the few one-story homes and parked across the street from it. Kendall stared at it wide-eyed.

"He lives with his father. His father's a piece of shit too. But, his father's truck isn't there. That means that Evan is the only one home."

I looked at the barely lit house. There was a small light on in the living room and a flickering light in one of the bedrooms. I immediately had a plan. I never thought that my messed-up childhood would ever come in handy but it was about to.

"Follow me. And be casual," I told Kendall before getting out of my truck and walking to the house.

I was surprised to see how willing Kendall was to go along with things. I was calm because of how many times I had done this. I didn't know what was fueling Kendall. Maybe it was vengeance. I would understand that.

"You gonna break down the door?" He whispered as we approached.

"No. There's a better way."

Walking up the driveway whose only light was from nearby homes, I looked around to see if anyone was watching and then stepped onto the lawn and circled the house. There weren't many trees so anyone staring out their window would see us. That wasn't a problem as long as we were quick.

"Don't touch anything. Nothing," I whispered.

I looked back to get his confirmation. He looked like he was about to throw up. I had no idea what was going through his mind. I partially expected him to call it off. He didn't. He wanted this as much as I wanted to do this for him. Approaching the backdoor and examining it, I looked at Kendall one last time.

"Are you sure this is the right place?"

"I'm sure," he replied shaking.

Taking out the gloves I kept in the truck and had stuffed in my pocket, I also pulled out my jimmy. It looked like something you would use to smooth paint or scrape the ice off of your windshield but was much better at prying open locked doors.

"Dogs?" I asked feeling the tumble slide back.

"I don't think so. He never had one."

When the latch became free and all that was left was to enter the darkness, I turned to Kendall one last time.

"Ready?"

He paused. Forcing a shallow breath, he shook his head.

This was it. Pushing open the door, I felt like I did every time I stepped onto the field. Everyone one of my senses was alert. My heartbeats echoed in my ears.

The place was dimly lit and cluttered. Kendall was right, a woman didn't live here. And following the smell of pot, I crossed the living room to the bedroom door with the light pouring out from under it.

Indicating for Kendall to hold back, I stared at the closed door then put my ear on it. I couldn't hear anything. What was he doing in there? It would make all of the difference. Had he heard us enter? Was he staring at the door waiting for us with a gun? There was only one way to find out.

Nothing beat the element of surprise. So, quietly grabbing the knob and crouching ready to pounce, I turned it, burst in, and then froze at what I saw. He wasn't getting high playing a video game. He was watching porn with headphones on and his hard dick in his hand. I couldn't have planned it better if I tried.

Seeing the movement in his periphery, he turned to find me. Stunned, he stopped jerking.

"What the fuck are you...," was all he said before I rushed him, grabbed his tee-shirt, and shook him like a rag doll.

He couldn't figure out what was going on. Letting go of his cock, the first thing he tried to do was pull his pants up. I found that hilarious. Rewarding his stupidity, I slapped him around. I made sure to hit him hard, though I'm sure it wasn't nearly as hard as Kendall had gotten over the years.

"What the fuck, man? What the fuck?" He babbled about to shit himself.

Sure that he was properly terrified. I stopped and pulled his face inches from mine.

"You piece of shit, you're gonna pay for what you did," I growled wanting to crush his skull like a melon.

"Who are you? I don't know you, man. You got the wrong person."

This was it. I had his attention. It was time.

"Come in," I said loud enough for Kendall to hear.

I had to give Kendall credit. When he stepped into the doorway, he entered like he wasn't scared shitless, which he had to be. Everything about him had told me that he wouldn't be able to do this. Turned out I was wrong.

"Kendall? What are you doing here?" He asked confused.

"Don't talk to me like we're friends, you piece of shit!" Kendall demanded. I was so proud of him.

"What are you talking about? We are friends. Tell him you know me. We're friends," Evan insisted.

"Friends? You think we were friends. You made my life hell for years. For years! You and your goon squad made me feel like crap every day of my life. The things you did to me…"

This guy's belief that everything was going to be alright slowly faded. Things were beginning to click for him. I was happy about that because that was going to make what I had to do next a lot easier.

"What I did to you? They were just jokes. We were just having a little fun. I swear," Evan said as his eyes bounced between the both of us.

"Constantly hitting me on the back of my head when you would walk by. Bumping me into lockers. Sticking my head in a toilet?" Kendall said with building anger.

"You came to school wearing makeup. What did you think we were gonna do?"

"There was shit in the toilet. You pushed my face into a toilet full of shit… and then you laughed about it!"

"It was a joke!"

Already on the edge, I couldn't hear anymore. I lost it. Turning him to face me, I made sure he was looking into my eyes before I pulled back my fist and let it fly. He didn't try to stop me or he didn't think to. And feeling the rage flow out of me, I beat him until my fists hurt.

I was out of breath when I let him go. He dropped onto the bed battered. I had made a mess of him, but it wasn't anything he wouldn't recover from. I knew how far to take things. I'd seen worse in the ring.

"Now," I said between pants, "You're gonna apologize."

"I'm sorry," he said looking at me like he was about to cry.

"Not to me you stupid piece of shit. To him."

He was scared to take his eyes off of me but eventually he looked Kendall in the eyes.

"I'm sorry," he mumbled.

"I didn't hear you," I growled.

"I'm sorry! I'm sorry, Kendall."

"For what?" I asked.

"For making your life hell. For being an asshole to you. For everything. I'm sorry for everything. I'm sorry, man. I'm just sorry," he said before bursting into tears.

I backed off of the asshole deciding that he got the point. I looked back at Kendall. I was amazed that nothing he saw had phased him. The man was stone-cold.

"What do you think? Do you think he meant it? Or should I beat the crap out of him some more?"

"I meant it. I swear I meant it."

"That's good enough," Kendall said relenting.

"Are you sure? Because I don't mind."

"No, please don't. Please don't," Evan begged.

"No. I think I'm good."

"Well, if you change your mind, just let me know. I'll come back and we can do this to him again." I turned to the guy in the bed. "Do you hear me? I could come back here at any moment for any reason, and you'll never be able to see me coming. Maybe I'll wait 'til you're asleep. Maybe I'll snatch you when you're going to your dealer. Or, maybe I'll send someone else. It might be anyone around you. It could be any time.

"And, if you tell anyone who did this to you or why… fuck!" I said with a laugh. "This is gonna be our little secret. You hear me?"

"I hear you. Our little secret."

"Good boy," I said tapping him on the cheek. When he flinched, I knew my job was complete. "After you, I told Kendall directing him out." I stepped back and looked at the guy on the bed one last time. "And, pull up your pants. Your dick is out." I looked down at it and laughed. That was when I exited, closed the door behind me, and then ran through the living room.

"Let's go," I said dropping my casual attitude.

Hearing my urgency, Kendall jogged behind me. Leaving through the front door, we hurried across the road to my truck, got in, and pulled off.

Neither of us said a word for miles. As much of a badass as Kendall was being, I knew it was an act. He wasn't that type of guy. He had probably never seen so much violence in his life.

I knew what I had done was wrong. Not for what I did to the waste of space I had beat the shit out of, but for what I did to Kendall. He would never be able to unsee what I did and he was never going to be able to look at me the same again.

"I'm sorry."

As soon as I said it, Kendall burst into tears. With his face buried in his hands, he sobbed. I had really fucked up. Like always, I had taken things too far. I had lost control and had made everything ten times worse.

"Listen, you shouldn't have had to see that. I lost control. It's just that, when you told me what he did to you, I got so mad…"

That was when Kendall sat up, crawled on top of me, and kissed me. My cheek, my chin, my lips. I was still driving. I wasn't sure what to do.

"Wait, I'm gonna pull over."

That didn't stop him. Even as I maneuvered to the side of the freeway, he was turning my face towards his. I could barely see as I brought the truck to a stop. And once I did, I pulled back the emergency brake and then did what I had been dreaming of doing from the moment I saw him.

Grabbing the back of his head, I pulled him onto my lap and pressed my lips against his. Parting them, I slipped my tongue in. My mind raced. In search of his tongue, I found it. They touched each other and danced. It was like nothing I had ever experienced. I was in heaven.

Pushing my fingers through his hair, I couldn't get enough of him. I wanted to be part of him. I wanted to feel his skin on my fingertips. So, sliding my free hand up his shirt, I traced the lines of his back. Touching him made me hard. With him sitting on my crotch, he felt it.

Grinding his crotch onto my stomach I felt his cock. He was hard too. I sunk my fingertips into his back when I realized it. I wanted him. I was ready to take him. And when he reached beside me and reclined my seat, I knew I was about to have him.

Pulling away from my lips, he kissed the bottom of my chin and my neck. Tilting my head back I gave him room. Nipping my neck and sucking on my Adam's apple, he pulled up my tee-shirt. It was enough for him to transfer from the dip in my neck to my bare chest.

He was slowly working his way down my body, and when he reached down and grabbed my cock, I returned my hand to the back of his head. I made clear that I wanted it if he did. Kissing and sucking further down my body, he unbuttoned my jeans. This was it.

His lips were on my belly button and his hands were about to reach into my pants and pull out my throbbing cock when he slowed to a stop.

"What's wrong?" I asked going out of my mind waiting for him to continue.

He didn't speak.

"What's wrong?" I insisted.

"Maybe I shouldn't," he said giving me no further explanation.

That was about to be the end of it. That was going to be all we did, until I cupped the back of his head, pulled his lips back to mine, kissed him, and then whispered, "Maybe I should."

Wrapping my arms around him, I spun him like I was running with the football. Working the cramped space, I placed him under me and high on the chair.

Pulling up his shirt, I quickly went to work. His chest was as smooth as I had imagined it. He had muscles but they were less defined. I liked everything about him.

Kissing his body, I took his nipple between my teeth. Applying pressure, he groaned. Wrapping my large hands around his narrow hips, I shifted him higher on the seat. I was a big guy and couldn't go much lower. At the same time, there was something else I wanted in my mouth. And when my chin touched his waist, I glided my hand over his clothed hard cock and went to work.

Unbuttoning and unzipping, I wiped my face across his bulge. This was Kendall I was doing it to. I couldn't believe it. He had to be the sexiest guy to ever live and I had him.

Taking a deep breath, I inhaled his scent. There was a hint of musk. It drove me wild. Not able to resist any longer, I pulled his pants down and revealed his shorts. I could see the outline of him clearly.

Overall, he was a small guy. His cock was not. I hadn't seen this coming.

Unwrapping my surprise and popping it out, I traced the lines of him with the tip of my nose. That was before I touched the ridge of his head with the tip of my tongue. That made him flinch. I liked seeing that so much that I did it again.

Taking hold of his thick manhood, I glided around him kissing every part of him. His body danced under my caress. Wagging my tongue up and down the base of his head, he lost his breath. So when I pushed his cock into my mouth, all he could do was grip whatever was around him and enjoy.

Massaging his balls, I did what I had thought about doing for so long. This wasn't just my first time doing this to Kendall. It was my first time sucking anyone off. I loved it.

I loved having another guy in me. I loved having control of his most sensitive part. And because it was Kendall, it was that much better. I would have stayed down there all night if Kendall's smooth body didn't stiffen into a plank and then explode into my mouth.

I allowed it to fill me and then swallowed it all. More than that, I sucked him dry. I couldn't get enough of him. I would have continued sucking him if he hadn't placed his hand on my head asking me to stop. It took everything in me to pull away, but I did.

Letting go but not wanting to leave him, I climbed up his body and held him. I never imagined being with a guy could feel this good. Holding Kendall, I knew I was home. I didn't want to be anywhere else but right here. I would have laid with him like that forever if he didn't then whisper in my ear.

Chapter 7

Kendall

"Thank you," I whispered unsure what I was grateful for.

Was it for what he had done to Evan? Was it for giving me the first, and most incredible sexual experience of my life? At that moment, I didn't know and didn't care. I just knew that I was bathing in warm caramel and I had never felt better in my life.

But, even though I didn't know why I said it, Nero thought he did.

"I'm glad you liked it," he said with a smile.

I was willing to let him have his ego boost. After all, the blow job was pretty great. I was torn whether or not I should ask him for another. Not at this moment, of course. Right now my brain felt like it was in a popcorn maker. Thoughts were bouncing around in my head faster than I could understand them.

I would have chosen to stay in Nero's arms a lot longer if flashing red and blue lights hadn't lit up the truck.

"Shit, it's the cops. Get back to your seat, Kendall. We don't what to have to explain what we were just doing to a couple of good ol' boys."

Knowing Nero was right, I pulled myself from under him and climbed into the passenger seat. He got back into his and returned his chair upright.

"Pull up your pants," Nero told me reminding me that my dick was still out. As I said, a lot was going on in my head.

I buttoned my pants and settled moments before a bright light filled the cabin. It was followed by a knock on the window and Nero rolling it down.

"What are you two boys doing out here?" The cop said from behind a glowing ball.

Nero replied.

"Are we not supposed to pull over here? I'm sorry, officer. I was feeling a little tired and I thought it was better to pull over than risk it."

The cop bounced his light between the two of us, then around the inside of the truck. When he didn't find anything, he turned it back towards Nero.

"You boys been smoking anything? You know, that stuff's illegal in the state of Tennessee."

"Wouldn't dream of it, officer."

"Then why does your truck smell like weed?"

"Does it?" Nero turned to me. "It must be on our clothes. We just left a friend. I don't want to get him in trouble, but we were in his room for a minute and there you go."

I couldn't tell if the cop believed Nero. The good thing was that Nero was telling the truth. That must have come across because, after only a few more dirty looks, he said,

"There's a rest stop five miles up ahead. If you need to rest, you should do it there. It's dangerous to pull over on the side of the highway like this. And, parked on the line like you are, you could cause an accident."

"Sorry about that. I didn't realize. We'll keep it moving from here on out. I just needed a minute to wake up. I'm better now. I can keep driving."

Still not hinting whether or not he believed us, the officer nodded and said, "Use the rest stops if you have to. Otherwise, you two have a good night, ya hear."

"You too, Officer. Thank you," Nero said as if he were the most polite person in the world.

"Thank you," I said as the officer walked away.

When he was far enough out of sight, we laughed. It had been a crazy night. We both knew to get home before anything else happened.

Just like the drive to Nashville, the drive back to campus was a quiet one. Probably for different reasons. Driving there my mind swirled about whether Nero was serious and what it might feel like to watch Evan get what he deserved. Driving back I couldn't stop thinking about Nero's lips on me and what it meant.

"Should I drop you off at your dorm?" Nero asked as we approached campus.

"It's pretty late."

"I reckin'."

"Maybe we could talk about things tomorrow."

"We could do that."

"Maybe we can grab dinner together again. You know, without the six-hour drive and other stuff."

"Without all of the other stuff? Because some of the stuff we did was pretty fun," Nero said blushing.

I couldn't deny that.

"We should talk tomorrow," I said leaving it at that.

"Okay. Just let me know if I can do anything for you. I'm more than happy to lend a hand."

"Or a few other body parts?" I asked blushing.

"Whatever you need," he said dropping me off in front of my building.

"Tomorrow?" I asked not really wanting to leave.

"Tomorrow."

I stared at him getting lost in his eyes. Perhaps I should have just opened my door and left, but instead, I leaned across the cabin, kissed him on the lips, and then hurried out.

I didn't look back. It was hard enough walking away from him. And when I say hard, I'm referring to my cock. There was a lot of time between him making me cum and me getting out of his truck. I was more than ready for round two.

Unfortunately, his spell on me only lasted a few minutes after I climbed into bed. It was past 2 AM so Cory was asleep. And it was way too dark and quiet for my mind not to return to what had inspired the night.

I couldn't believe that I had watched Nero beat the crap out of Evan. As I thought about it, my body shivered. I don't know why, but as soon as that happened, I melted into a crying mess.

Eventually crying myself to sleep, I was only awake for a minute before the tears began again.

"You okay?" Cory asked startled by the sound of me wailing.

"I'm... all... right," I said through my sobbing.

As hard as I've always been to live with, I never felt sorrier for Cory than I did now. At least previously I could explain why I woke up screaming or chose not to leave my bed. Today, I couldn't even do that. I was crying. That was that.

Of course, as the day continued and the spontaneous bouts of bawling carried on, I got a better sense of why it was happening. These weren't tears of anger or frustration. They were from a soul-felt release. These tears were from all of the times I hadn't cried as a kid.

For so long I had thought that Evan Carter wouldn't get justice for the things he had done to me. I knew that an eye for an eye left everyone blind. But, why was I supposed to be okay carrying around the terror and pain he inflicted on me while he got away without consequences?

Before last night, I didn't believe that fairness existed. Because it didn't, God couldn't exist and there was no way life could be trusted. We were just specks of nothing floating aimlessly in a void of emptiness. But that had changed.

As brutal as it was, Nero had given me hope that everything might be alright. Helping others to have a better life would be worth it. What you put out to the world came back to you. I hadn't needed proof of this to want to be a therapist, but knowing there was justice in the world had changed my life.

With every tearful outburst, my life felt a little lighter. And by the time I met Nero for dinner, I was practically giddy with happiness. I was pretty sure he thought I was high.

"You high?" Nero asked right on cue. "Because if you are, why aren't you sharing?"

"No, I'm not high. I just feel different."

"Really? The blow job was that good, huh?" He said looking proud of himself.

I didn't want to burst his bubble.

"You're a miracle worker."

"Then maybe we should do that again."

"Maybe we should," I said thinking it wasn't a half-bad idea.

"Want to get out of here?"

"I didn't mean now."

"What then? In five minutes? You want us to leave separately so no one knows what we're doing? There's a bathroom two floors down. I could meet you there. It wouldn't even be an issue."

I laughed.

"I'm serious."

"I know you are. That's what makes it funny," I said reaching over to his chair and placing my hand on his arm.

I liked touching him. Doing it filled me with a warmth that told me that everything was going to be alright.

"No, Nero. You did what you did for me last night and I appreciate it."

"You're welcome," he said again referring to his blow job.

"Not that! I'm talking about the other thing."

"Oh."

Reminding him of it took a bit of the wind out of his sail.

"That."

"Yeah, that," I confirmed.

"I'm just glad I could help you get what you deserved. Honestly, after the things you described, I don't think a beating and his apology is enough."

"It's enough. Besides, that wasn't the only thing that happened. You gave me my life back. I was stuck in that nightmarish loop and it warped the way I saw everything. You straightened it out for me. It was more than any therapy ever could."

Nero's head dipped sheepishly.

"I'm just happy I could do that for you, ya know?"

"You're an amazing guy, Nero Roman. And now it's my turn to help you."

"I'm pretty screwed up. You're not gonna be able to beat someone up for me and make it all better like I did."

"I don't know. I'm pretty strong."

Nero laughed.

"Hey, it's not that funny."

"I know. I know. You're pretty strong. But maybe you leave the fighting to me."

"Whatever," I said with mock frustration.

Holding the joke for a moment, we both laughed.

"No. I think the way I can help you requires more lips than fists."

"Oh definitely. That's gonna help a lot!"

"I meant talking."

"Oh, that."

"Yes, that. Maybe you can tell me what's bothering you."

"Right now, I'm good. Believe me, sitting here with you, I couldn't be better."

I had to admit that that felt pretty good to hear. But he wasn't going to sidetrack me with sex… as great as that sounded.

"Okay, so you're good right now. But, what about when you smashed up that car? And how did you know how to get into Evan's house? And, why are you so good with your fists? Something tells me they're all linked."

Nero stared at me not giving an inch.

"Come on. The only way you were able to help me was that I was willing to open up to you. It might not have seemed it, but that wasn't easy for me. You now know more about what happened to me than anyone outside of the people who were there.

"If I'm gonna help you, you're gonna have to let me. I want to do this for you, Nero. But, you have to let me in."

Nero's jaw tightened. His head drooped.

"If you wanna know the truth, then here it is. Let's start with why I smashed up that car."

"Okay."

"I did it because of you."

"What?"

"It was after you told me to go fuck myself."

"I didn't tell you to go fuck yourself."

"That's what it felt like," Nero said drowning in pain.

"I'm sorry about that. It was shitty of me even if you now know why I said it. There's no excuse for it."

"No, I get it. If what happened to you happened to me, I would feel the same way."

"I don't feel that way anymore, though," I said touching his muscular forearm again.

"I'm glad," he said offering me a gentle smile.

"Here's the thing, though. What I said was bad. It was. But what about it made you go video game on a car?"

"I don't know."

"Come on. I'm sure you can give me some idea. Before you did it, were you thinking of anything? Did something else flash into your mind?"

Nero thought about it. "Something did."

"Good. What was that?"

"My father."

"Okay. What's your father like?"

"I wouldn't know."

"Why not?"

"Because I never knew him."

"So, you and Cage grew up with just your Mom?"

"Cage and I met less than a year ago."

"Is he a half-brother?"

"No, we're full brothers."

Trying to work it out, I got very confused.

"You're gonna have to explain it to me. I'm not putting it together."

Nero leaned back and then told me about the last year of his life. He told me how Quin and Cage found him and where he was when they did.

"So, you organized fight clubs?"

"It was the only way I knew how to make money."

"How do you make money running fight clubs?"

"By betting on yourself," he explained.

"Got it."

"I didn't like doing it. Okay, sometimes I did. But, I also had a shitty busboy job because I was trying to find a way out of it."

"So, the anger you feel?"

"What about it?"

"It's because you grew up without a father?"

Nero looked at me and again leaned back.

"Ya know, Cage and Quin just got the keys to their new place. They're gonna be moving my mother in this weekend. They need me to move my stuff. How would you feel about going up with me? That way I don't have to explain everything. You could just see it."

I froze not expecting this. It felt like such a loaded question. Did he realize that he was asking me to meet his mom? And, what about the sleeping arrangements? Was he doing this with the hopes that we would have sex? Did I want to have sex with him? Was I ready to have sex?

"Um…"

"It's okay if you don't want to," he said trying to hide his disappointment.

"I didn't say that."

"So, you want to."

I grunted torn. "Can I think about it?"

"Of course."

"Maybe we should grab something to eat. I'm feeling pretty hungry and the café is closing soon."

"We should do that," Nero said seeming much soberer than moments ago.

Once the mood changed, it never went back. After we were done eating, I got out of there by saying I had to get up early for a class. I told him I would give him an answer to his invitation in a few days, and I was going to. I just needed to figure out everything about him and where I wanted the rest of my life to go, first. No problem.

Between jacking off to the memory of Nero sucking me and classes, the week flew by. As the weekend approached, I still hadn't come any closer to a decision. Because I hadn't, I was hiding from Nero. I didn't mind sending delayed responses to his texts. But I wasn't yet ready to see him.

Thinking a change of scenery would help, I took a walk around campus. Nearing Commons, I decided to browse the bookstore within. It mostly sold textbooks, but occasionally they'd have something worth me buying to pretend I've read.

Walking the aisles, I stopped with a jolt when I saw someone I recognized. Quin was staring at the crafts supplies with his back to me. I wondered if I should say hi and decided it couldn't hurt.

"Quin?"

Quin turned around and stared at me with a confused look on his face.

"Kendall," I reminded.

"Yeah," he said awkwardly.

As he continued to stare at me without saying anything, I began to think I made a mistake.

"We watched the football game together. We got pizza afterward. It was fun."

"Oh, I'm sorry. Yes, I know who you are. Cage says I have a tendency to stare without saying anything. I guess I keep expecting people to read my mind," he said with a chuckle.

"No worries," I said feeling the awkwardness fade. "You look like you have something on your mind."

"Yes, I do. Do you know what a moonshine festival is?"

"Isn't it a pagan ritual type of thing?"

"No. The other moonshine."

"Ah yes. A Tennessee specialty. Moonshine, I mean. What about it?"

"Snow Tip Falls, the town where Nero grew up, is having their first annual Moonshine Festival. And since I am becoming a part of the community, I thought I should volunteer to do something big."

"What did you do?" I asked seeing where this was going.

"I volunteered to be the mascot."

I put my hand over my mouth. "You didn't."

"I did. And I said I would make the costume."

I stared at Quin and then burst out laughing.

"Why on earth would you volunteer to do that?"

"I'm the new guy in town. Besides, everyone's been so welcoming to Cage and me that I wanted to do something to say thank you."

"And nothing says thank you for not being homophobic pricks like dancing around in an oversized, uncomfortable costume all day while kids laugh and point."

"The town's not like that. It really is quite nice. In fact, the only problem we've ever had was with Nero and now he's head over heels for a guy."

"He is? Who?" I said feeling an unexpected rush of jealousy.

"You." Quin stared at me blankly. "Wait, did you not know that? Did I say something I shouldn't have?

Oh, I'm sorry. Forget I said that," he said starting to panic.

"No, no. You didn't speak out of turn. He's made his feelings clear. I guess I just have a hard time believing that someone like him could be interested in someone like me."

"Oh. Yeah, I had the same feeling about Cage."

"I hope you don't mind me saying this, but they are two pretty hot brothers."

"No, I don't mind. It's hard to miss. So, does that mean that you're into Nero as well?"

I took a deep breath unsure what to say.

"Who knows? I'm such a mess. But you, what are you planning on doing for your moonshine mascot outfit?"

"I was thinking about making a mason jar. I mean, that's what they would drink moonshine out of back in the day, right?"

I winced. "It's more what fancy restaurants serve drinks in now-a-days to fake a downhome vibe."

"Is it?"

"Your New York is showing, Honey."

"Is it? Then what do I do," Quin asked frantically.

"Why don't you just do a moonshine jug?"

"What's that?"

I looked at Quin stunned. "What did they even teach you in high school?"

"Math," he said dryly.

I laughed.

"Touché. Well, now that you're in Tennessee, you're gonna have to go back and learn the fundamentals."

I tried to explain what a moonshine jug looked like. By the time I got to the part about there being three Xs on the front of it, he was lost.

"Why are there three Xs on it?"

"To tell people that they will die if they drink it. Moonshine's grain alcohol. It'll burn your insides out."

"But people do drink it, don't they," He asked confused.

"Of course. What else are you gonna do with it?"

"Make a car bomb?" He asked wryly.

I laughed hard. "That's only after you've drunk it."

"Okay, so it's clear I need some help with this," he said defeated.

"I could help you."

"You could?"

"Sure. I mean, you clearly need help and I've made enough wire-framed dresses to fill a festival."

"Why would you make wire-framed dresses?"

"I went through a rebellious phase," I explained. "I thought I could bring couture to Nashville. FYI, I didn't."

"Oh, do you want to be a fashion designer?"

"No, a therapist."

"Which also makes sense," Quin said considering it.

I stared at him speechless. I didn't know if he was being funny on purpose or not, but the guy was hilarious. I really liked him.

"So, did you want my help creating your masterpiece?"

"You don't know how much. And just so you know, a masterpiece would be great. But I'm aiming for not humiliating myself."

"Well, you'll be dressed as a moonshine jug at a small-town festival. So, Quin, that ship has sailed," I said sympathetically.

It was Quin's turn to laugh.

With a project to take my mind off of Nero and whether I would join him this weekend, I led Quin out of the bookstore. Since neither of us had cars, we walked to the nearest art supply store. Picking up framing wire, reams of cloth, paint, and sewing supplies, we took a rideshare back to his dorm.

The guy didn't live like the rest of us. He lived in the building jokingly referred to as Beverly Hills. Spreading everything out in his living room, I showed him a few pictures of what I was thinking of and got to work. It was fun. And it turned out to be a great way to pick his brain about Nero.

"So, what did you mean when you said that Nero was the only one who gave you and Cage a hard time?"

"Nero wasn't always as in touch with what he wants as he is now. And, things might have come out a little wonky."

"He was a closet case?"

"Yeah. I guess."

I thought about that a little more.

"He has a temper, doesn't he?"

Quin's eyes flicked up to mine. He didn't need to say anything. The answer was clear.

"He's had a hard life."

"He's mentioned something about that."

"I think if Cage hadn't come along, his life might have led down a dark path. It's difficult growing up without either of your parents."

"I thought he said he grew up with his mother."

"He did. She was physically there. But, in all of the important ways, he was alone. She had a rough go of things, too. She's only now returning to her full self."

"Wow!"

"Yeah. So, he might be a little angry and rough around the edges. But he was exactly how strong he needed to be to survive the world he was forced into.

"And the more I get to know him, the more I see how he uses his darker side. Nero is a protector. He looks after his pack. If you're on the outside, you better watch out. But, if you're one of those he lets in, you are the safest you will ever be."

I thought about what Quin said throughout the rest of dinner. It made sense. Wasn't that what happened with Evan? Hadn't Nero done what he had to protect me?

"You should come check out the festival," Quin said as we approached a stopping point for the night. "You're doing all of this work. You at least need to see me humiliate myself in it. Cage and I just got a place. We have an extra bedroom if you want to stay over."

"Oh, Nero mentioned that you and Cage bought a house. Congratulations on that."

"Thanks. And we have plenty of room for guests."

"Nero had actually invited me up this weekend to help him move in."

"Oh!" Quin said looking at me surprised. "Did you say yes?"

"I told him I had to think about it."

"You should do it… if you feel comfortable. I mean, do whatever you'd like. You'd be very welcome if you do. You've met Titus. He'll be in town, too. It should be a fun time."

"It could be," I said feeling very tempted.

Agreeing to come back the following day to help him finish his costume, I headed back to my place. I was pretty sure if Nero hadn't invited me first, I would have already accepted Quin's invitation.

It wasn't that I didn't want to spend time with Nero. I absolutely did. I wanted more of what we did in his truck.

But, that was the problem. The reason I was in his life was to help him, not help myself to him.

What if I let myself fall for him? There would be no coming back. How could I resist him? Not only was he as hot as sin, but I liked everything about him.

And, Quin was right. When I was with him, I felt safer than I had ever been in my life. That wasn't saying much considering the hell Evan and his asshole friends had put me through every day at school, but it meant a lot to me.

"Cory, I have a dilemma," I told him when I arrived home finding him still awake.

"Boy problems?" He asked putting down the textbook he was reading.

"How did you know?"

"Kendall, you've been glowing the last couple of days."

"I have?"

"Did you not know?"

I thought about it. Despite how stressed I had been trying to figure out what I should do about Nero, I had been drunkenly happy.

"Maybe."

"At least, you've seemed happier than you've been the two years I've known you."

"I guess. But, I wouldn't describe it as boy "problems". I just can't figure out what I should do." I paused. "Wait, are you comfortable talking about this?"

"Why wouldn't I be?" Cory asked confused.

"I don't know how you straight boys work? Maybe this grosses you out or something."

"Kendall, we've been living together for years. Do you really think you talking about something that has made you happy could gross me out? What is it that you think of me?"

"I don't know. I guess I just get freaked about this stuff sometimes."

"Fuckin' Evan Carter," he said waiting for me to follow it with my line.

"About that…"

"What?"

"So, I might have gotten closure on the Evan Carter situation."

Cory sat up giving me his full attention. "How?"

"Did I mention there's a boy?"

"I don't understand."

"If I remember my behavioral psychology class, I might have had something called, Learned Helplessness. It's when you give up because you've decided that there's nothing you can do to escape the bad situation you're in.

"If you put rats in a cage and electrify the bottom of it, eventually they learn they can't escape the shocks so they stop trying. So when you only electrify the small section they're standing on, they won't move. They've learned they're helpless to escape their situation even though they're not.

"That might have been what had happened to me with Evan Carter. His constant bullying had taught me that I had no control over my life and that I was helpless to all the bad things that could happen. I was stuck in mud. The boy helped me out of it."

"How'd he do that?"

"He beat the shit out of Evan Carter," I said worried what Cory would say.

"Oh!"

He leaned back and went silent.

"It's wrong, right?"

"Well, it's not like he didn't have it coming. He did some shitty things to you."

"I haven't even told you the humiliating stuff."

"There's more?" He asked stunned.

"Yeah. He was…"

I had to take a deep breath when the memories flooded my mind.

"He was the devil," I decided.

"And, after this guy did what he did…?"

"I feel better. I don't feel scared all the time anymore. I feel like I can breathe for the first time in a long time."

"That's great!"

"Yeah. But…"

"But what?"

"I don't know. Should I be worried? I mean, I met him because I'm supposed to be helping him adjust to school. And, the reason I was asked to do it was because he's had some anger issues. Couldn't all of this be dangerous?"

Cory thought about it. "Do you feel like you're in danger?"

"That's just it. I feel incredibly safe around him. I feel like, if I'm with him, there's nothing that can hurt me because he will protect me."

"Wow! That's pretty amazing. Who wouldn't want that?" He said with more introspection than I would have expected.

"So, I take it that being with your girlfriend doesn't make you feel safe?"

Cory looked up at me and laughed. "Well, my girlfriend is a girl who's smaller than me, so no."

"What does her being a girl have to do with it?"

"You know, a guy is supposed to protect the girl he's with. That's probably what she's looking for from me."

"But there are other ways a person can make you feel safe, right? Like, maybe she makes you feel safe because you know that she will be there when you need her. Or, maybe she makes you feel safe because you know she will always love you."

Cory looked at me considering it for the first time.

"I guess. Wow! You're really good at this."

He couldn't have said anything nicer. I blushed. "Thank you. So, does she make you feel safe in any of those ways?"

"Maybe."

I stared at him as his eyes saddened.

"But those aren't the ways you want to feel safe. Or, maybe that you need to feel safe?"

"Look Kelly's a great girl!" He said defensively.

"I didn't say she wasn't."

"And, we weren't talking about me. We were talking about you. Don't try to change the topic."

I guess I touched a nerve.

"You're right. We were talking about what I should do about Nero. So, my dilemma is that he's going home this weekend and he invited me to go with him."

"He wants you to see where he grew up. That's a good thing, isn't it?"

"I guess."

"And he wants you to meet the people who are important to him. To me, that seems like he's taking things to the next level."

"Actually, I've already met a few of those people. I was just helping his brother's boyfriend put together a costume for a festival his town is hosting this weekend. It's their place we would be staying at. And Quin invited me to come up for the weekend, too."

"This all sounds fantastic."

"Does it?"

"Yeah. The guy invited you to learn more about him. And because his brother's boyfriend also invited you, the pressure would be off from it being a date. By the way, his brother has a boyfriend?"

I smiled. "I guess hot and gay runs in their family. Although, I think they both might be bi."

"They're bisexual?" Cory asked with more interest than I was willing to dive into right now.

"You should meet them. They're pretty cool… even though they're football players."

"They're football players?"

"Yeah," I said with a smile.

"Kendall, I don't even know who you are anymore."

I laughed. "I'm not sure I do either."

"But, I think you should go. I've known you for a while. I've never seen you this into something, much less someone. What if he's your chance at happiness?

Wouldn't it be worth taking the risk… even if there might be a few complications?"

Chapter 8

Nero

I was going out of my mind waiting to hear what Kendall decided. I had invited him back to Snow Tip Falls. Everyone I ever knew was there. If he was with me, I knew I wouldn't be able to hide how much I liked him and they would see it.

And, what would my mother say? She had no problem with Cage and Quin, but she had been introduced to them as a package. If she wanted to have her son back, she was going to have to accept both of them. Now, I wonder if she likes Quin more than me.

But, unlike the two of them, my mama's known me my entire life. I've never given her or anyone reason to believe I could be into guys. This was going to be a complete surprise to her.

And what would everyone else I knew say? I didn't exactly hang with the most enlightened people. Things could turn bad quickly. I knew I could shut anyone up who stepped out of line, but that didn't mean it wouldn't bother me.

At the same time, I was helpless to Kendall. I could barely breathe when I was around him. All I could think about was holding him, and pushing myself into him with my arms wrapped around his chest and my lips on his neck. I have never been more turned on by someone in my life.

That could have been what was behind my recent play. Or, maybe it was that I now had a reason to leave it all on the field. I wanted to impress Kendall. I wanted him to see that being with me would be worth it no matter how fucked up I am.

But, hell, maybe that was just a dream. Maybe I was too fucked up for anybody. Meeting Kendall had made me hope that I was wrong. I was willing to risk everything to be with him. All I needed was for him to text me back and give me that chance.

I was starting to think that Kendall was gonna ghost me when a picture appeared in our text thread. It was of him and Quin standing in front of what looked like a human-sized moonshine jug.

Nothing about the picture made sense. I knew he and Quin had hit it off. But when did they start hanging out together? And why was there a giant moonshine jug in Quin's living room?

'How much of that moonshine did you two drink?' I wrote back.

'Well, we had to empty the bottle, so…'

I was still very confused.

'Do you need someone to walk you home? Because I'm close.'

A picture was the next thing to appear. This time the two of them were pretending to be drunk as they drank out of the jug. They were clearly having a good time.

'You know that stuff will make you go blind, right?'

'lkajfoi ; al;keaa alk;edfa ;lka,' he wrote back.

I laughed.

'Seriously, do you need me to come over? I'm five minutes away.'

'No. We're good. I just wanted to show you the costume we made for the Moonshine Festival this weekend.'

'The Moonshine Festival?'

'You know about it?'

'Know about it? I've been roped into helping set it up. You commin', by the way?'

'Quin said they have a spare bedroom I could stay in.'

Reading that, my chest clenched. I had hoped he would want to sleep in my bed. There were a whole lot of things I wanted to do to him.

'They do. You should come!'

Those three dots danced on the screen for what felt like forever.

'Ok'.

"Yeeeessss!" I screamed causing Titus to look over.

"Get some good news?"

"It wasn't bad," I told him unable to wipe the smile off my face.

"Are you going to Dr. Sonya's festival this weekend?"

"I'll be there." I paused not sure how to bring this up. "And, ah, you remember Kendall?"

"From after the game?"

"Yeah. He's coming too," I said nervously.

"Is he? That's great! I liked him."

"Maybe you can get Lou to come?"

"I asked him. He has a date this weekend."

"He dates a lot, doesn't he?"

"He does."

"I didn't realize there were so many gay guys at East Tennessee."

"There aren't. When he can't find one, he converts them," Titus said with bite.

"That bother you?"

"Why would it bother me?" Titus asked playing dumb.

I stared at him wondering if I was going to keep dancing around what was going on between the two of them.

"Look, if you like him, I think you're gonna need to step up and tell him."

"I don't like him! I mean, I like him. We're good friends. But, I don't like him like that."

"Huh! Well, I guess it's a good thing you don't. Because if you did, hearing he's going on yet another date might drive you up the wall. Imagine all of the things he does with these guys. Imagine them holding hands. Imagine them kissing. Then when they invite him back to their place…"

"He's a virgin!" Titus said cutting me off.

"What?"

"Yeah. He said he dates a lot but he doesn't go any further than that. He wants to wait for the right guy."

"Was he looking at you when he said it?"

"What do you mean if he was looking at me? He was talking to me. Of course, he was."

I stared at him wondering how long he was gonna play this game.

"Okay. Whatever. I just think if you feel something for someone, you need to tell them no matter how chicken shit you are?"

"You tell Kendall that?" He asked throwing it back in my face.

"I'm gonna tell him this weekend," I said coming out to the guy I was gonna see every single day. I guess it was official. There was no turning back now.

"Good for you!" Titus said looking at me with admiration. "That's awesome. He seemed really nice. I like you two together."

"Thanks," I told him filling with relief.

Not having a game this weekend, Kendall and I made arrangements to meet at Quin's room so the three of us could drive to Snow Tip Falls together.

"So, neither of you thought about how to get it through the door when you were deciding how big it will be?" I asked staring at the four-foot-wide jug costume.

Kendall and Quin looked at each other. It was the cutest thing ever.

"Okay. Here's what we're gonna do. Quin, you're gonna take all the pictures you want with it looking as perfect as it does right now."

"And then?" Quin asked nervously.

"Then, we're gonna get it through the door."

"Oh no! We put so much work into it," Quin moaned. "I haven't made anything like this before."

"Then maybe next time you two will make something smaller than the doorframe you need to get it through. Weren't you supposed to be a genius or something?" I teased.

Quin's head drooped. I don't know why, but that might have taken things too far. I put my hand on his shoulder.

"Look. I got you. We both got you. Right, Kendall?"

"Of course. We got you, Quin."

"I just wanted Cage to see it at its best."

"And he will… in the pictures," I said teasing him again.

Quin's mood lightened allowing him to laugh about it. I did the same. But when I looked over at Kendall, I caught him staring at me with a big grin.

"What?"

"Nothing," he said before turning his attention to the costume.

I didn't know what he was thinking, but I liked the way he looked thinking it. He really was the sexiest guy ever. Damn, did I want to kiss him again.

After taking more pictures than a tourist at Tennessee's biggest ball of yarn, Quin put his camera away and we got to work. Having made it strong enough to trap a bobcat, the only way we could get it through the door was to bend it. When we got it to my truck and bent it back, it was more oval than round.

"It's a Moonshine Festival. If people are sober enough to notice it's a little off, then we got bigger issues," I told a sad Quin.

As much as I liked being alone with Kendall, having Quin with us for the drive to Snow Tip Falls helped. The two of them got along like best friends. I was a little jealous. But, just when I thought they forgot I was here, Kendal touched my thigh. I had never gotten hard so fast in my life.

I turned to him wondering what he was suggesting. He wasn't looking at me. It was like he just wanted to tell me that he hadn't forgotten about me. I was gonna take it, because I certainly hadn't forgotten about him.

By the time we were pulling up to our new home, Kendall and I were introducing Quin to Tennessee drinking songs. Were we singing loud enough to wake people up as we drove by? Probably. But there's only one way to sing a drinking song and it ain't quietly under your breath.

"Is this your house?" Kendall asked staring through the windshield in awe.

"Yeah," Quin replied bashfully.

"It's amazing!"

"Thanks."

Yep, there was no getting around it. The place was impressive. I wondered what Kendall would say when he saw where we were moving out of. I hadn't been embarrassed about my place growing up because I didn't have the time to be. I was too busy figuring out how to pay the rent.

But, I saw the neighborhood the kids from his school lived in. None of those homes were on wheels. Sure, none of the homes in our trailer park was either. But that was because no one there could afford them.

"Nero, after we get the costume inside, you should show Kendall around."

Kendall turned to me excitedly. "Cool."

"Is Mama here?" I asked Quin wondering how stressful my night was going to be.

"We special ordered her bed. It's arriving tomorrow. She won't move in until then."

I was relieved. It would give Kendall and me a night to get used to whatever was going on. Once we moved the costume into the garage and said hi to Cage, that was what we did.

"They told me that this would be my room," I said guiding him in and onto the bed.

"Nice!" He said looking around at the empty space.

"We're getting my stuff tomorrow. But I'm not sure how much of it I wanna bring with me. Maybe it's better to let most of it stay in the past."

"You can't beat a fresh start."

"Yeah."

I stared into Kendall's soft, chocolate eyes. It was like he was asking me to pull him into my arms and never let him go. But, as soon as I slipped my hand on his, he stood up.

"So, where's the room I'll be staying in?" He asked grabbing his backpack.

I considered suggesting that he stay with me, but changed my mind. I wanted him to feel comfortable here. And if he needed to sleep somewhere else to do that, I would give that to him.

"Next door. I'll show you."

Allowing him to drop off his stuff, he told me that he would meet me downstairs and then closed the door behind me. How could I not take that as a rejection? He may as well have said, "Don't let the doorknob hit ya on the way out." I was starting to think this weekend wasn't gonna go like I hoped it would.

"Where's Kendall?" Cage asked when I joined him and Quin at the kitchen island.

"He's in his room. He said he'll be down soon."

"So, how's it going between you two?" Cage asked.

I nodded my head and tightened my lips instead of answering. The truth was I didn't know.

"You guys got anything to drink?" I asked checking the cabinets.

"First of all, it's, do *we* have anything to drink?" My brother said referring to the three of us. "And second, of course," he said before pointing me to a lower cabinet.

I opened it and stared at the sorry selection.

"You know this ain't gonna do, right?"

"You want more? You go buy it," Cage joked.

"No. I'll stock it up," Quin volunteered.

"Now, why aren't you more like your boyfriend?"

"Not all of us can be perfect," he said grabbing Quin and kissing him.

"I don't know who you're talking about. But, I know it's not me," Quin protested.

"Of course it's you. It's always you," Cage said being so cute with Quin that I wanted to puke.

"Where the hell is Kendall?" I asked not able to take it anymore. As soon as I said it, Kendal walked in as if he was waiting at the door. "There you are," I said not able to stop myself from smiling. "Drink?"

"My God, yes," he said joining me and pointing out what he wanted.

Once the drinks started flowing, things between Kendall and me got less awkward. Sitting at the island as Cage made dinner, the conversation was non-stop and pretty great. When we were done, Kendall and I cleaned up and then joined my brothers in the living room. They had bought a second set of games for the house and Kendall and I challenged Cage and Quin to a game of Wavelength.

The object was to come up with a word that would get your teammate to turn a dial to a certain area without seeing it. It was basically testing which team was on the same wavelength. Cage and Quin crushed it. But considering how well we did against the perfect couple, neither Kendall nor I felt bad.

"We're gonna head to bed. We have a lot to do tomorrow. Don't forget that after we move, we have to help Dr. Sonya set up for Sunday."

"Got it," I told Cage waving him off.

When they were gone, I turned to Kendall. God, did he look sexy.

"So, what about you? What do you wanna do?"

He stared at me for a moment and smiled.

"I think I'll head to bed, too."

"You sure? I could think of a few other things," I said with a smile.

"I'm sure you could. Maybe next time slugger," he said before leaning over, kissing me on the lips, and walking away.

I barely knew what to do with myself for the rest of the night. Deciding to go to bed, I stared at the wall knowing he was on the other side of it. I tossed and turned restlessly before I took things into my own hands and relieve some of my stress. It was only then that I could think warm thoughts of Kendall and slowly drift to sleep.

I woke up early the next morning not being able to stay away from Kendall for very long. Lying in bed, I stared at the wall separating us. Was he awake staring back? If he was asleep, what was he dreaming of?

Way too antsy to stay in bed, I pulled on a pair of shorts and left my room. His door was still closed. Convincing myself not to knock, I headed downstairs finding Cage and Quin in the kitchen.

"Morning," Cage said as if he had been awake for hours.

"Mornin'."

"How did you sleep?" Quin asked. "Was the bed comfortable? We debated about how soft it should be. Cage said you wouldn't care."

"He doesn't know how uncomfortable the bed back at the old place is," Cage told me.

"Yeah. Anything would be an upgrade from that," I agreed trying not to take my brother's criticism personally. "But it was all we could afford, you know."

"Hey, for a place that was being paid for by a fourteen-year-old, it's amazing. I still can't believe you were able to do it," Cage told me. "But, it's not just you anymore. We're all in this together. And now we have a new home."

"Yeah," I said half-heartedly.

I knew Cage was trying to make me feel like this was my place too and I appreciated it. But, it wasn't. I didn't think it could ever be. It was too big of a leap from the place I could afford. You could fit the mobile home in it multiple times. It was too different from everything I've ever known. How could I not feel like a guest?

"Is Kendall still sleeping?" Quin asked.

"I guess. He took the guest bedroom."

"Oh. Cage was wondering if he should start making breakfast. Do you know whether he's a late sleeper?"

"I wish I knew that type of information," I said hoping that I would know it soon.

"Okay. I'll give it a few minutes and then get started. It'll take a while in either case. Maybe he'll be up by then."

"While you do that, I'm going to take a shower," Quin said kissing Cage before he left.

When Quin left I looked at Cage. I tried to think of the last time the two of us were alone together. The only times I saw him nowadays was when he came to campus and stayed with Quin, or when I drove Quin up for the weekend. I loved Quin, but I kind of missed spending time alone with my brother.

"How's work going?"

"Good! I'm loving working with the kids. I keep trying to figure out when I can invite you to a game but you either have practice or classes."

Cage refilled his coffee cup and offered me some.

"Please. And things have been good with Mama?"

After he handed me a cup, he joined me at the island.

"Yeah. I mean, you've seen her. She's even been talking about going back to work."

"She told me. It's amazing. Where was this woman when I was a kid?"

"She was doing her best."

"Don't defend her. You weren't there. You don't know what it was like," I said.

I wasn't upset, but there was no way I wanted to listen to him make excuses for her while only seeing her good side.

"Sorry."

"You ever wonder about our father, Cage?"

"Of course. You know I do."

"Quin tell you what he decided?"

"What he decided?"

"Yeah, I had asked him to help me figure out who he was. And he told me that I might not want to know."

"What does that mean?"

"I don't know. He's your boyfriend."

Cage's gaze dipped as he thought about it.

"What if our father is someone really awful, Cage? Like, what if the reason Mama doesn't want to talk about it is because if we knew, it would explain why I'm so screwed up?"

"I don't know, Nero. But, do you think we need to know? I mean, we have Mama. We have each other. Maybe that's enough."

"Quin thought you'd say that."

"Did he?"

"Yeah. But, I don't know if it's enough for me. It's like a missing piece in my life. All I can ever think about is why our father wasn't around.

"Was it because he didn't know I existed? Would he want to know? Did he know and not care? And, why was it that Mama refused to talk about it? What is so bad about me that she can't bring herself to say?"

"Have you ever asked her," a new voice said from the kitchen doorway.

I turned to find Kendall. How much had he heard?

"Oh, hey. You're up?"

"Yeah, I've been up for a bit. But, I heard what you were saying to Cage. Sorry, there's a bit of an echo in here."

"The rest of the furniture should be delivered in a couple of days," Cage explained.

"You heard everything we were saying?" I asked.

"Just the part at the end about you needing to know about your father."

I lowered my head. I didn't have a problem telling Kendall stuff which was amazing, considering. But, admitting what I had to anyone other than someone in the same boat, was pretty hard.

"I've been asking my mother about my father my entire life. She's never been wanting to say anything about it."

Kendall entered the kitchen and stood within arm's reach. "Did you tell her how important the information is to you?"

I looked at Cage not sure how to respond. I wasn't ready to tell Kendall that Mama had gone insane for a few years and hadn't given a shit what was important to me.

"I think she knew," I told him.

"She might have. But sometimes saying the words changes things."

"Maybe," I said thinking about the words I would use when I told him how I felt about him.

"It might help. And, if you need any help with it, I could talk to her. I haven't met your mother yet, but sometimes it's easier to talk to a stranger."

I didn't think anything he said would work, but I thought it was sweet of him to offer. I took his forearm in my hand. His smooth skin glided under my slowly circling thumb.

"I appreciate you offering. But, maybe you should meet my mother first."

Kendall's confidence quickly vanished. "Yeah. Of course. I didn't mean to…"

"You didn't do anything wrong," I said cutting him off. "It's just that, our mother was dealing with stuff as I was growing up. So, she wasn't much for talking. She's doing a lot better now. So, maybe things are different. Hell, maybe if I asked her again now, she'd tell me."

"You never know," Kendall encouraged.

"You never know," I agreed.

Cage spoke up. "You know how I feel about this. But, Kendall could be right. Sometimes it's easier to talk to a stranger."

"I'd be more than happy to."

I turned to Kendall. He looked like he really wanted to do this for me.

"If it comes up. But, please, Kendall, don't push it."

"Of course. Only if the moment's right," he said with an excited smile.

I stared at Kendall trying to figure out why something like this would make him happy. But, it did. There was still a lot about him I didn't know. He was like a gift I couldn't wait to unwrap.

"I'll get started on breakfast," Cage said leaving the two of us.

He was probably starting to feel uncomfortable. I was staring at Kendall pretty hard, and he was staring back at me just as much. God damn did I want to kiss him. And when he suddenly lifted his hand and rubbed a finger across my naked chest, I almost lost it.

I leaned forward to reach his lips when he pulled away from me. What was he doing? You couldn't tease a snake like that. You were gonna get bit.

To make his point further, he joined Cage and offered to help him with breakfast. I didn't chase after him because my dick was too hard. I couldn't get up.

Instead, I watched him cross the kitchen collecting the ingredients as my brother whipped up a feast. Kendall was fitting right in. There was something sexy about that that made me want him even more.

After eating way too many pancakes and bacon, Kendall joined me as I cleaned up. When we were done, we all got dressed and got ready to do some packing. Cage and I drove separate trucks to our old place. The first thing I was going to have to do once I got there was introduce my Mama to Kendall. It was freaking me out a little.

Parking, I felt like I was getting ready to play a big game. My heart was pounding. There were no stopping things now. I didn't know what I was going to say. How was I even going to introduce Kendall? As much as I wanted him to be, he wasn't my boyfriend. But, just calling him a friend didn't seem right either.

Kendall must have picked up on my anxiety because before we got out of the truck, he took my hand and squeezed it.

"You can do this," he told me.

"Do what?"

"I don't know. Whatever it is that's got you so stressed."

"My mother doesn't know I'm into guys. I know that we aren't anything yet…"

"We're something," he said cutting me off.

"What are we?"

"We're friends."

"Just friends? Because the things I wanna do to you aren't the things I wanna do with someone who's just a friend."

I waited wondering if what I had admitted would freak him out. I expected him to tell me we were nothing at all.

"We're *good* friends," he said with a smile.

"You know I wouldn't mind us being more, right? I really like you, Kendall. I've never liked someone so much."

I stared at him. I had poured out my heart. Why wasn't he saying anything?

"I…" he said fading off.

"I helped Mama pack most of her stuff yesterday," Cage said approaching my window. "We'll donate most of the kitchen supplies to Goodwill. Mama's okay with it. But if there's anything with sentimental value, you should get it now."

I didn't know if Cage had saved me from hearing Kendall tell me he wasn't interested or not, so I wasn't going to complain about his interruption.

"You got it, Bro," I said gazing into Kendall's eyes for a moment longer. "You ready to meet my Mama?"

For the first time, Kendall looked nervous. "Yeah."

Catching up with Cage and Quin as they entered, we poured into the space proving once again that our family had outgrown the place.

"Hey Mama," Cage and Quin said with each of them kissing her.

"Mama, I want you to meet someone," I told her trying to breathe.

She turned to me. Her eyes quickly jumped to Kendall.

"This is Kendall. He's, ah, he's someone very special to me, Mama."

Mama looked at Kendall.

"Is this your boyfriend?" She asked taking things further than I expected.

"No. But I'm hoping one day," I said not realizing how much I was putting Kendall on the spot.

Mama got up and approached Kendall.

"It's very nice to meet you, Kendall," she said before offering him a hug.

That stunned me. She barely gave me hugs. I couldn't remember the last time she had given me one. I was beginning to realize that I didn't know who my mother was. For most of my life, she had been the woman on the couch mindlessly staring at the TV. Was this who she had been before whatever it was that had changed her?

"It's nice to meet you, too," Kendall said hugging her back. "Are you excited about moving?"

Mama let him go. "Oh yes. Very excited."

"This place hasn't been so bad, has it, Mama?" I asked feeling a bit of a sting.

"This place has been our home. But, it's time to put this part of our life behind us. We could all use a fresh start. Don't you think?" She asked squeezing my hand with a smile.

Although I didn't answer her, I knew she wasn't wrong. It was time for all of us to move on. What did that mean in my case? How much of my future involved Snow Tip Falls? If I declared for the draft, I could end up on a team on the other side of the country. Was I really gonna return here in the off-season?

"What here do you want me to pack?" Kendall asked when we retreated to my room.

I looked around at the space that was barely bigger than my bed. Anything that had meant something to me I had brought with me to my dorm.

"I think I'm gonna throw it all out."

Kendall turned to me surprised. "Everything?"

"Yeah."

He looked around, pulled a yearbook from a shelf, and flipped through it. "Even this stuff?"

"Get rid of everything. Mama's right. It's time for a fresh start."

I don't know why but Kendall rubbed my back and rested his head on my shoulder. I wasn't complaining. It felt nice. I wanted more of it. But, I was pretty sure he was doing it because he thought the junk around me meant more to me than it did.

What I saw when I looked around was the place I returned to the time I got my face bashed in after being caught stealing. Or, the room where I cried my eyes out when my mother stopped speaking for a month. I had been terrified she would never speak again.

"They could burn this shit as far as I'm concerned," I told him grabbing a handful of crap and tossing it into a box.

Once I decided that, packing took no time at all.

"Where's the pile for the dump," I asked pushing out four full boxes.

"All of it?" Cage asked.

"Everything."

Cage looked behind me at Kendall. I turned around in time to see Kendall shrug. I didn't know what to make of the two of them but it rubbed me the wrong way.

"You guys need any help packing up the rest of this shit?"

"We're getting through it okay," Cage explained. "Was there any of this that you wanted to keep?"

"No. I don't think my lucky spatula is in there," I told him feeling done with the place. "If you don't need us anymore, I think we'll take off. I'm gonna show Kendall a bit of the town."

"Are you still planning on helping Dr. Sonya set up for the festival?" Cage asked.

"Yeah. I'll head over this afternoon."

"Quin, are you gonna need help with the costume?" Kendall asked.

"Not today. I'm good. You two have a good time. Snow Tip Falls is beautiful this time of year. You'll love it, Kendall," Quin said with a smile. "Hiking the falls was one of our first dates."

"And then you fell through the ice and we had to rush you to the doctor," Cage said with a laugh.

"Oh, right. I forgot that. Whatever you do Kendall, don't walk on the ice in someone's footsteps," Quin said with a smile.

Kendall looked at me confused. "Are we going to be walking on ice?"

"Don't pay attention to him. That was just a city boy learning a little backwoods lesson," I teased. "We'll catch up with y'all later. I'll take these boxes to your truck."

After Kendall and I carried the last of my old life out, we got into my truck and took off.

"So, where are you taking me to?"

"How do you feel about hiking?"

"Well, I'm wearing my hiking boots," he said with a smile.

I looked at his feet and saw he was wearing his usual black Doc Martins.

"You bin hiking before?" I asked confused.

"Hiking? Pfff. When have I not gone hiking?" He said sarcastically.

"You've never been hiking, have you?"

"In my defense, hiking gets you all sweaty…"

"And?"

"It gets you all sweaty. That's enough."

I laughed.

"Well, there are places I want to show you, but it might require you to get sweaty to get there."

"So, you want me to get all hot and sweaty with you. Is that what you're saying?"

"That's exactly what I'm sayin'," I said loving his suggestion.

"We'll see tonight. Until then, how about you show me this place you're excited about," he said with a flirtatious smile.

"You sure you could take it? The hike, I mean."

"You'll just have to take it easy on me because it's my first time."

I paused wondering what he was referring to.

"Wait, you've never… "hiked" before?"

"Never."

"Have you?"

"I grew up here so I've hiked a few times. But, I've never hiked with someone like you before," I told him hoping we were still talking about the same thing.

"So, if we hiked together, it would be the first time for both of us?"

"Yeah, I guess. But, I've thought about hiking with someone like you plenty. And, you're the type of guy I'd like to hike with for the rest of my life."

"How would you know? We haven't even hiked for the first time yet."

"Because I've never wanted to hike with someone more."

Kendall stared at me. "I just want to be sure. We're both talking about sex, right?"

"I was."

"So, you've never been with a guy before?"

"No. But, the thought of being with you… it keeps me up at night."

Kendall slid closer to me on the bench seat and put his hand on my thigh. He looked at me for only a second and then returned his gaze ahead of us.

"I'd love to see whatever you want to show me," he said turning a shade of pink as he did. "But, in time," he clarified.

"When you're ready."

"Thank you," he said moving his body against mine and getting comfortable.

With him next to me, I was tempted to never stop driving. I loved the feeling of his touch. Unable to resist, I wrapped my arm around him pulling him even closer. Just the smell of him made me hard.

I also wondered if he would start kissing me again. He didn't. This time we drove together as if he were already my boyfriend. I wasn't sure why he kept touching me like he liked me, yet would never say anything when I told him how much I liked him. Maybe he was hesitant. But, he was gay. Why would he be the hesitant one, when I was the one who had to step off a cliff to be with him?

I didn't know, but whatever I had to, I was willing to do it to be with him. And, if that meant taking things slow, then I was good with that. Maybe "good" was the wrong word. But, I would do it.

Deciding that I wanted to show him more than just a beautiful hike, we drove out of town for thirty minutes. When we pulled over, it was at the edge of a lake.

"We're here."

Kendall peeled himself off of my chest and sat up.

"Where are we?"

"We are the furthest I'd ever been from home before I went to East Tennessee University."

Kendall gave me a confused look and then scanned the lake more intensely. I was fine to stay in the truck and look at it from here, but he got out. Joining him I could tell there was something on his mind.

"What is it?" I asked guessing what he would say.

"This was the furthest you had ever been."

"Yep."

"Did you come here fishing?"

"Nope."

"Then, what brought you?" He said moving in front of me.

I looked at him and then stared at the lake. It had been a long time since the last time I was here. The memory of it made me uneasy but I had always known it was something I would have to deal with.

"I know my mother seems fine now. But, when I was a kid, there was a time when she shut down."

"Oh no!"

I looked at Kendall. I appreciated his sympathy.

"Yeah. She stopped working. Eventually, she stopped paying rent. When the rent collector would come sniffing around, we would pretend we weren't at home. But one day he caught me and told me if we didn't pay by the end of the week, we would be out.

"I told Mama but it was like she didn't hear me. It probably made her slip away even further. But, knowing I was the one who would have to do something, at the end of the week I went to find him.

"I explained to him that I didn't have the money but I was willing to do whatever I had to pay the rent. He looked me over and then told me he could give me a job to work off our debt. Desperate, I agreed.

"It turned out that our trailer park wasn't the only one he owned and he hated having to collect the rent. He said that my job would be to collect the money people owed him and I was supposed to get it no matter what."

Kendall took my hand. Maybe he knew where my story was going.

"The first person he told me to collect on, I did what I was told. I ended up having to track down when the guy was home. When he was, I went over and banged on his door. I felt awful for doing it. I knew how this guy felt. But I screamed at him to give me what he owed the guy. The only thing he said was for me to go fuck myself.

"What was I supposed to do? I tried, he wouldn't give it to me, so I went back and told my landlord what happened. When I was done, he walked up, looked down at me, and slapped me across the face. He hit me so hard he knocked me to the ground."

"Oh no!"

"Climbing on top of me, he started punching me. I didn't know what was going on. I hadn't even been in a fight before. And he was a big guy. His rings were cutting into my face.

"When he was done, he got off of me and said,

"You want your ass to be out on the street? You want your Mama to start whoring herself to take care of you? Because I'll take it that way just as easy."

"I screamed, "Fuck you!" I kept screaming, "fuck you!"

"Then you go back there and collect my fuckin' rent, he said. And don't you fuckin' come back here until you have it. You hear me?"

"I knew what his beating was. It was a lesson. He was teaching me what I was supposed to do. I was supposed to collect the money or beat them senseless until I got it.

"I wasn't gonna do that. I couldn't. So, instead of returning home, I ran. I thought if I could get far enough away, I wouldn't have to worry about anything anymore. So, I kept running and running. I didn't know where I was going, but eventually, I ended up here, looking out at that," I pointed at the lake.

"Why did you stop?" Kendall asked.

"It was cold and I couldn't figure out how to get around it. I knew which direction I was heading in, but I didn't know how big the lake was. I ended up sleeping under a tree because I couldn't decide what to do next.

"When I woke up was when I considered what would happen to my Mama if I kept going. She had nobody and could barely take care of herself. Maybe he would make her whore herself to keep living there. I imagined him sending men to where we lived and them doing things to her. I couldn't let that happen. I had to protect her from that."

"So, what did you do?"

"I went back. I didn't even go home. I walked right back to the man who owed the guy rent. This time I didn't knock, I broke the door in. Finding him hiding in the back room, I did what I had been taught to do. I beat on him until he gave me everything he had.

"Taking it, I told him when I would be back for the rest. When I gave it to the guy, he was impressed. And at the exact time I told the man I would be back, I went and collected the rest. My mother and I didn't have to pay rent after that. I just had to make sure that everyone else paid their rent, and I did."

When I was done with my story, Kendall looked at me stunned.

"How old were you?"

"Fourteen."

When I said it, he burst into tears. He didn't say anything more. He just wrapped his arms around me and cried.

I thought I could tell him this and let it go. I had needed to get the story off of my chest. It wasn't something I felt comfortable telling Cage, and until now, I didn't have anyone else.

But, I hadn't expected all of the tears. Hearing Kendall whimper made me consider why he was. I had never allowed myself to think it was a big deal but there was no escaping it now. The man holding me was telling me how big of a deal it was. He was right. And the more I realized it, the less I could hold myself together.

Listening to him cry, I slowly broke down. All of the pain I had been running from rushed to the surface. It was like a dam had broken. I couldn't turn off the waterworks. Eventually, the weight of it brought me to my knees.

Still not saying anything, Kendall kept holding me. It just made me cry more.

"I didn't want to hurt all of those people," I tried to tell Kendall. "I was just a kid."

"You were just a kid," Kendall repeated. "You had no other options. You were just protecting the person you loved."

My heart burst realizing that Kendall understood. I didn't think anyone would forgive me for the horrible things I had done. But, Kendall did. And for the first time, I felt that maybe I wasn't alone.

It took a long time for either of us to stop crying. Once we did, we sat quietly for an hour. When my butt became sore, I thought about my promise to help Dr. Sonya set up for the festival. I wasn't sure I was in the mood for it. I had told everyone I would, though. So, gathering my strength, I cleared my throat.

"We should go back. I told Dr. Sonya…"

"We don't have to. We can stay here as long as you'd like."

"No, I said I would. Besides, I think I'm losing feeling in my ass," I told him shifting and making a face.

Kendall tried to resist, and then laughed.

"I lost feeling in my butt thirty minutes ago. I don't think I can move my legs," he said humorously. "Didn't you say something about hiking? You didn't warn me about sitting on the ground. I don't have nearly enough padding for that."

"Hey, I like your ass. Don't you be talking bad about it," I said with a smile.

"Then you can have it. I would much prefer to have yours."

"Don't you go tempting me like that unless you mean it!"

"You know what I meant," he said with a smile.

"Yes, I do. That's why I was warning you."

Kendall looked at me with playful frustration and fought his way to his feet. He was as shaky as a fawn walking for the first time. It was adorable.

"Alright, come here," I told him picking him up and carrying him.

"That's okay. I got it."

"No, no. If you're gonna listen to my long story and sit there while I cry about it, the least I could do is carry you to the truck."

Giving in, Kendall wrapped his arms around my neck and relaxed.

"If you insist."

"I do," I said looking into his big brown eyes.

As I looked at him, he reached up and kissed me. It wasn't a long one, and when I tried to make it longer, he leaned back. Carrying him, I had no way of reconnecting with his lips. Placing him on the passenger side of the truck, he scooted away from me. I was starting to believe that he was teasing me on purpose.

Driving back to town Kendall explained how much my experience had shaped my life.

"I think that's why you destroyed that car. It's because, at a young age, you learned that violence is the solution to all of your problems."

"Isn't it, though? Violence paid my rent. Not only that, it got me my football scholarship. And wasn't it my violent tendency that won you? Let's face it, violence is what gave me everything that means anything to me."

He paused. I had him. At least, I thought I did.

"It's not your violence that got you your scholarship. I've seen you play. You've gotten what you have because you're good, and you're fast. How many hours have you spent working on that? It was your hard work that got you that."

"What about you? Wasn't it what I did to that asshole that got you to think about football players differently?"

He was quiet again.

"It's okay if it did. I'm used to it."

"But I don't want you to be. I don't want you to think that that's the way to solve your problems. You smashed up a car. Look where that got you."

"Smashin' up that car got me sitting here now next to you," I said with a smile.

I was very happy to have won this debate, but not as much as Kendall hated losing it.

"Kendall?"

"Don't talk to me."

"Come on, now. Don't be like that. Ya can't always win an argument."

"You think I care about winning an argument?"

"It really seems like it from where I'm sitting," I said unable to contain a smile.

He looked at me frustrated.

"Well, I don't. I don't!" He yelled getting upset.

"Alright, alright. No need to get a way about it."

"You don't understand. If you think the way to solve every problem is with violence, what happens the day I become the problem you have to solve? Will you do to me what you did to Evan?"

"What? No! Why would you even think that?"

"Isn't that what you were saying? Weren't you saying you have a violent nature and that violence got you everything important to you?"

My face went white hearing his words. I felt like throwing up. The only thing I could do was pull over and shut off the truck. I turned to him quickly and he flinched. He thought I was going to hit him or something. As soon as I realized it, I raced out of the truck and emptied my breakfast into the weeds.

The retching didn't stop. Every time I thought it was done, I would picture him flinching away from me and I would dry heave again. Eventually, Kendall came over.

"Are you alright?"

"I would never do anything like that to you," I told him in the middle of convulsions. "Never! You gotta believe me. I wouldn't!"

"Okay, I believe you," he said kneeling next to me and rubbing my back. "I'm sorry I let you do what you did to Evan. I can see now that I wasn't helping you by letting you do it."

"I did it, not you. You didn't let me do anything."

"I gave you his address. I practically drove you there and sicced you on him. It was just that I was so angry."

"So, now you know how I felt," I said looking at him. "When I act like I do, it's because I get so angry. But, I know that one day you're not gonna find someone to beat me up no matter what stupid thing I do. Just like there is nothing I would ever do to hurt you."

"But, how do I know that?" He asked sincerely.

"You're gonna have to trust me."

"For me, trust is hard," he explained. "It's not like guys like you have given me any reason to."

"And it's not like anyone in my life has given me a reason to trust them. But, I'm willing to trust you. I don't know why, but I am. I'm asking you to do the same."

Chapter 9

Kendall

I stared at the man in front of me. He was not who I thought he was. When I first met him... well, I couldn't remember our first meeting. But when I saw him by the pond, all I could see was how gorgeous he was. He may as well have been a picture in a magazine. That's why it was so easy to dismiss him when I found out that he was a football player.

When I was introduced to him as my client, or whatever he is, I saw him as a hot bad boy. But what did that even mean? Who did I think I was talking to?

Standing over him as he wiped the puke from his mouth, I realized that I didn't know who he was. Telling him that I was scared of him hurt him so much that he tossed his breakfast. Who was capable of such sensitivity?

Built like a Greek statue, I assumed that he would be the strong one. And, maybe he is, but it isn't in the way that I thought. Sure, he could pound a guy like Evan

Carter to mush. But he was also capable of trusting me when every moment of his life had taught him to trust nobody.

That was his true strength. In that way, he was stronger than me. How could I not love that about him? How could I not love him for it?

Oh shit! I love him for it. I'm in love with Nero, my football player client. What was I supposed to do now?

"I trust you," I told him. "At least I'll try too. Nero, you're the most unexpected guy I've ever met."

"Thank you?" He asked looking at me confused.

"I don't know if it's a compliment as much as it is an admission that you aren't like anyone I've ever met. And because you're not, I have to consider you without weighing you down with my baggage."

"I don't know what that means."

"It means… I don't know what it means other than that I think you're special."

"And, because you're smiling, I'm assuming you mean it in a good way and not the way a teacher tells a parent that their kid is special?"

I laughed.

"No, I mean it in a very good way. You are… pretty great," I said feeling my face get hot.

"Okay, I could work with that. I think you're pretty special as well. It's more in the parent/teacher way. But that could be good, too."

I hit him on the shoulder in jest and he laughed. "Come on."

"No, I'm kidding," he said getting up. "I think you're pretty great, too."

He took my shoulders in his hands and looked into my eyes. Staring up at him, my heart thumped. I started to lose my breath. I had to swallow.

I wanted him. I wanted everything about him. I wanted him in me. I was about to lean forward and get it until he said,

"Um, I would kiss you right now. But I just spent the last little bit…." He pointed at the remains of Cage's pancakes."

"Right. Maybe we should head back to town. Weren't we supposed to help set up for the festival?"

"I know I was. But no one roped you into doing it. You don't have to feel obligated."

"Is that where you're gonna be?" I asked.

"I guess so."

"Then, that's where I wanna be."

Nero smiled as much as I was. More than that, my dick was hard. That wasn't that unusual considering how often thinking of him made me take things into my own hands. But there was a reason I was still a virgin.

I wasn't a complete idiot. I could tell there were guys who wanted to stick their junk in me. A few of them were even hot. But, I never felt it with any of them.

I felt it with Nero. Why was that? Could it be because he was the first guy I ever felt I could trust?

With him still holding my shoulders, I placed my palms on his chest. I had just wanted to touch him, but once my hands were there, it was hard to miss his muscles. It felt amazing. Mesmerized by the feeling, I looked down and slowly explored the ripples. He stood taking it for a second until,

"Ah, unless you have something very specific in mind, you should probably stop that and we should go."

I looked up unsure why he had said it. He pointed down at his pants. It took only a glance for everything to become clear. Nero was not only hard, but the guy was huge. And, when he flinched, it sent a pulse through me that made me weak in the knees.

"Yeah, we should go," I told him with a swallow.

Driving back to town I couldn't help but touch him. It was all that I wanted to do anymore. With his arm around me as we drove, he told me stories about when he was growing up. I got the feeling that he was avoiding the horrible stuff. But what he told me gave me a clear picture.

Since the age of fourteen, Nero had been living a double life. Not wanting people to know what was going on with his mother, he didn't tell anyone about his after-school job. He went to classes and football practice, and then once he got off, he became the rent collector.

He talked about how much of an effect it had on him.

"When did you realize you liked guys?" I asked him.

"If I look back on it, I probably always knew. But, it became pretty clear after puberty. There were boys at school I couldn't stop thinking about. There were a few girls too, but it wasn't the same. I used to fantasize about jacking off with guys even though there weren't really any of them I thought about kissing. But there weren't too many girls either."

"So, have you been with any girls?" I asked unsure if I wanted to know the answer.

"A few. But, you know how it is. You get drunk at a party after a game, and a girl throws herself at you. Before you know it, your dick is in her and it's all over."

"Yeah, I don't think I know how that is," I said with a laugh.

"Have you ever been with a girl?"

"I haven't been with anyone."

"Have you gotten close?"

"I think the closest I've gotten is with you," I admitted shyly.

"Why is that? Only a blind man can't see how hot you are," Nero said with a blush.

"Thank you," I said feeling his compliment. "I guess I never saw myself that way."

"Because of that asshole?"

"Who? Evan?"

"Was that his name?" Nero asked getting mad thinking about him.

"Yeah. It could have been because of him and the rest of them. I don't know. I just know that I wasn't willing to make myself vulnerable like that before now."

"Before now?"

I looked up at Nero. "Yeah."

I could feel Nero's body heat through both of our shirts. His smell was all around me. Still staring up at him, I lost all of the resistance I had towards him and slipped my hand on his inner thigh. Liking what I was doing, he helped by spreading his legs.

Sliding my hand further, I felt his clothed balls. I couldn't believe I was touching it. As soon as I did, it wasn't enough. Cupping them in my small hand, I squeezed. He groaned.

That was all I needed. Moving my hand to his cock, I followed the length of him. I had never touched another guy like this. It made my head spin it felt so good.

Not stopping there, I turned around and unbuttoned his pants. Still driving, he scooted forward allowing me to unzip him. Sticking my hand past his waistband, I found his hard flesh. I was touching his cock. Pushing my fingers further onto him, I wrapped my palm around it. He filled my hand.

Unable to wait a second longer, I freed the length of him and pulled it out of his underwear. Even with him seated, he was huge. Needing to get my lips around him, I leaned down. That was when he pulled the truck to a stop and gave me a better view. He was the biggest guy I had ever seen. And with both of my hands holding him, I bent down and kissed his tip.

Feeling my lips on him was electric. But that was just the start. Allowing my tongue to escape, I tasted him. He was tangy.

Pushing his head into my mouth, I bathed him in my warm saliva. He moaned liking it. So when I pulled back allowing my lips to ride his curves, all he could do was bury his fingers in my hair and enjoy.

With him gently tugging at me, I lowered my head pushing the tip of him onto the back of my throat. I didn't choke like I always imagined I would. So, with it sitting there, I pushed harder.

It was a weird sensation when my throat opened up allowing him to slide in. He had seemed so big, and he was. But he fit in me and I could feel him go deeper.

It sounded like Nero could breathe as little as I could. And when I pulled back allowing my throat to snap shut behind it, we both inhaled sharply.

"Jesus!" Nero exclaimed sounding like he had just seen him. "Where the hell did you learn to do that?"

I chuckled and returned to giving the man I loved the experiences of his life. Twirling the tip of my tongue around the ridge of his head, I stroked his shaft with both of my hands. It was like gripping a small baseball bat. I could feel his veins as I did. This was what I had always imagined sucking a guy would feel like. Getting more comfortable by the second, I threw myself into it until he was deep inside of me again.

Tugging and sucking, it wasn't long until his grip on my hair tightened. He was coming. I wanted him to shoot it down my throat. When he was flinching uncontrollably and leaning back, I pushed him as far into me as he could get. I could feel his twitching as he unloaded. It was unlike anything I could have imagined.

As Nero loosened his grip on me and I ran out of breath, I retreated and sat up. Nero looked like he had seen god. He was happy. I loved that. When our eyes met, he smiled.

"Thank you!" He said before he touched my face. "Your eyes are watering."

"I wonder why," I joked.

Nero laughed allowing his head to roll.

"Seriously, Kendall, where have you been my whole life?"

"Waiting for you."

He looked at me and then laughed. I couldn't tell if he was giddy or drunk.

"I'm falling in love with you, Kendall. And what you just did isn't helping."

Did he say that he was falling in love with me? I wasn't ready to hear that. Sure, I was already in love with him, but if I admitted it, it would put us in a place I wasn't prepared for. Instead, I reached up and kissed his cheek followed by his chin and Adam's apple.

I didn't want him to think that I didn't love him. I did. It was just that it wasn't time yet. I wasn't sure why not, or when it would be. But, I wasn't going to tell him I love him sitting in his truck with his cum working its way down my throat.

"Oh fuck! We're here!" I exclaimed as I took my eyes off him to find parked cars and a field full of people. "I thought you had pulled over to the side of the road again."

"Yeah, I was gonna tell you that. But then you stuck my dick in your throat and I lost the ability to speak."

"Do you think anyone saw us?" I asked embarrassed.

"I parked back here hoping no one would. But even if they did, they would have only seen me. Besides, you don't know any of these people."

I scanned the area. We were as far from the field as you could get. Even if they did see us, they probably couldn't make out what was going on.

"Relax! Like I said, no one here knows you."

"That doesn't mean I don't want to make a good first impression."

"Fair enough. But I've met you. There's no way for you to do anything else."

I turned to him and smiled. "You're very sweet. Now pull up your pants. I'm the only one who needs to be seeing that."

"So pushy!" He joked before sitting up and returning his monster to its cave.

Driving the truck closer, we parked and entered the field. Looking around, it felt like the day before a festival. Booths were being set up and there were a lot of people around. Everyone was walking casually except for one person. When she spotted Nero, she hurried over.

"Good, you're here," the fair-skinned, mid-fifties woman said in a slight Jamaican accent. "I thought you weren't going to make it."

"Sorry we're late. Something came up that Kendall had to take care of."

The high-energy woman turned to me. "I assume you're Kendall? Dr. Sonya," she said offering her hand.

"Nice to meet you. I heard that you're the one organizing everything. It has to be a lot of work."

Dr. Sonya gave an exaggerated look of exhaustion. "You can't even imagine. But you're both here now. Are you ready to roll up your sleeves?"

"Definitely," I said enthusiastically.

"Good." She turned to Nero. "I like this one. Now, both of you get to work. Look for Titus. He knows what I want you to do," she told us before hurrying off.

"She seems nice."

"Don't let her fool you. Let your guard down and she'll have you volunteering to paint the town red."

"I think the town would look good red," I joked.

"See! She's already got you," he said with a smile.

I wasn't sure who Titus was, but when I saw him, I recognized him.

"Kendall, right? Nero told me you were coming," Titus said with a glowing smile.

"You remember my roommate, right?"

"Oh, I didn't realize you two were roommates."

"Yep! He can't get rid of me," Titus said playfully.

"Speaking of that, is Lou coming?" Nero asked with a smile.

"How are those two things connected?" Titus asked confused.

"I don't know. Is he?"

"He is not. Busy this weekend."

"A shame."

"Yeah. Anyway, Dr. Sonya has assigned you the task of putting out the welcome signs," he said referring to a box beside him. "There's one that hangs across the street. That one should go at the beginning of town."

"Do you mean at the general store or something?"

"I trust you to figure it out," he said patting Nero on the shoulder with a smile. "Also, there are a few signs with arrows. We've gotten permission from the school to use a few of their sawhorses. Make sure people know how to navigate here from the main road."

"Is there anything else she wanted us to do?" Nero asked sarcastically. "I'm sure we'll have the time."

"I hear she was looking for someone to paint the town red?" I joked.

"What?" Titus asked confused.

Nero laughed. "Don't worry about it. We'll take care of this. I'll call you if we run into problems."

"I knew I could count on you," Titus said flashing another winning smile.

I had never helped set up anything like this, but what Nero implied was right. It was a lot of work. It wasn't like it was hard. It was just time-consuming.

First, we needed to go to the school and find the handyman. But, he hadn't heard anything about us picking up the sawhorses, so then we had to find the principal and find the handyman again.

After that, we had to figure out how to attach the signs and where to put them. Although we had more than enough signs, we only had three sawhorses. That would have been fine if there were only three turns. But, there weren't so we had to get creative.

Once that was done, we unfolded the one that was supposed to hang over the street. The thing was huge and was meant to hang from ropes. Okay. But what did the ropes attach to?

We spent an hour trying to figure out how to hang it between the general store and the empty lot that was across the street before we gave up. We then considered hanging it between the store and the restaurant next to it, but decided that it would be too low and that no one would see it.

It wasn't until the sun was setting that Nero got the idea to hang it a mile out of town. There was only one road that led into Snow Tip Falls. On either side of it were trees. And halfway down it was the remains of a wall.

The entire area use to be the compound for a community of moonshine runners. Hence the festival. The dilapidated wall was the remnants of that time.

"So, there are definitely places we can hang it from," I said looking up at the pine trees. "And it would be high enough for people to see and drive under. But, how are we supposed to get up there?"

"How are you at climbing trees?" Nero joked.

"Great! Good thing I wore my climbing boots."

"I thought you wore your hiking boots?"

"And I thought you were taking me hiking, but plans change," I said teasingly.

We had a lot of other ideas about how to hang a twenty-five-foot sign between trees twenty feet in the air. None of them were good. As it got dark and we got desperate, Nero decided to do the obvious, climb the trees.

It was impressive. I wasn't an outdoors type. So, to see him get physical with nature gave me thoughts.

"I'm gonna lower the rope and I need you to attach it to the sign," he told me as it came down.

"This probably wasn't the best plan," I told him tying it off.

"I'm open to suggestions if you have a better idea for the other side."

"Oh, and is there a knot you can use for us to pull it from side-to-side to center it?"

Even in the dark twenty feet below, I could see the glare Nero gave me.

"Sorry! You're doing great!" I said giving him an enthusiastic thumbs up.

He stared at me for a second then went back to work.

When we were done, we hadn't done a half-bad job.

"I like it!" I told him. "Good job!" I said hugging him from behind.

He wasn't quite as excited about it as I was. He was more bruised and covered in pine sap. He looked exhausted. He didn't even have the strength to thank me.

Returning to the truck we drove back to their place in silence. I didn't think he was mad at me. But, unsure, I gave him his space. Parking, I followed him into the house and joined Quin, Cage, and his mother at the kitchen island, while Nero continued upstairs.

"Hey! How did it go?" Quin asked me cheerfully.

"It was an interesting day."

"Where's Nero?"

"Washing off the interesting day, I'm guessing."

Quin laughed. "Something to drink?"

"Absolutely. By the way, should I worry about him?"

Cage replied. "Did he go silent?"

"Yeah."

Cage shrugged. "Just give him a few minutes. I'm sure he'll be down when he's ready. Meanwhile, I'll start dinner."

The cider I was handed made it a lot easier to relax. As the alcohol kicked in, I joined in on the conversation. After everything Nero told me today about his mother, I saw her differently. It was hard not to see his upbringing as abusive.

She was clearly going through a mental health crisis with no one to help her. It was an unfortunate situation for everyone involved. But I couldn't help but take Nero's side.

Despite that, I tried to be as friendly as I could and make the best impression I could on her. She was still the mother of the guy I was in love with. No matter how I felt about her, she would never stop being that.

"Nero said that you're thinking about going back to work. Do you have any idea what you would want to do?"

"I don't know. Whatever's available."

"I told you, Mama, you don't have to take just anything. I can take care of you. If you want to work, find something you'd enjoy doing," Cage insisted.

"That's not the way it is around here, Cage. This isn't New York. You take the work you can find."

"No one's mistaking this for New York, Mama. Quin?"

"Not me," he joked.

"See. And all I'm saying is that you don't have to go find something that will make you unhappy. You can take your time. Figure out what you want to do. When you have, go do that."

She shook her head as if trying to get used to the idea. "That's not the way it worked in my day."

"We get that. But you have two sons now."

"I've got three sons," she said looking at Quin.

"Thanks, Mama," Quin said.

"Which reminds me, when are you two going to make things official?"

Quin and Cage looked at each other.

"In time," Cage said with a smile.

"It's wonderful seeing how much you accept Cage and Quin being together. I'm not sure my parents would be so accepting."

"Your family would have a problem with us?" Nero said joining us in the living room. He wasn't wearing a shirt. It looked like he had just gotten out of the shower.

As drool-worthy as he looked, I hadn't missed that Nero had referred to us as if we were already a couple. I ignored it.

"They didn't have the easiest time dealing with me. I liked pushing people's limits. Theirs included. And, the more anyone resisted, the harder I pushed."

"How did that work out for you?" Nero asked.

"I got my ass kicked every day. But what else was a boy as pretty as me supposed to do in Nashville?" I said flipping my head pretending to have long hair.

Everyone laughed except for Nero. I had said what I had to be funny. I guess it wasn't once you knew the details.

"Dinner's ready," Cage said sending us to the dining room table.

With the drinks flowing, everyone's mood improved. Even Nero's. Sitting next to me, I spent the whole night thinking about his hand on my thigh. I would say that it's hard to eat when you were this aroused, but it wasn't. I probably ate more compensating for what I couldn't put in my mouth.

Following dinner with a rousing game of Scrabble, Quin was wiping the floor with us without trying. After he put down an eight-letter word that more closely resembled Roman numerals, I questioned him about it.

"If you want to challenge it, you can," Quin offered.

"Don't do it," Cage joked. "He's memorized the Scrabble dictionary. If he puts it down, believe me, it's there."

"You memorized the dictionary?" I asked stunned.

"I mean, not the whole dictionary. It's more about learning the words that help you place the hard-to-play letters. There are only a few dozen of them."

"And by a few dozen, he means about five hundred," Cage explained.

"Seriously?" I asked amazed.

Quin shrugged.

I looked over at Nero who said, "You can challenge him, but I've learned my lesson."

"We all have. But be our guest," Cage explained.

"Yeah, Kendall. Be our guest," Quin said with a cocky smile.

"Wait, are you doing smack talk?" Nero teased. "Has Quin started doing smack talk?"

Quin blushed.

"Okay. I give up. If Nero tells me to trust you, I will. I'm not getting anywhere near whatever you all have going on," I said playfully.

"Smart move," Nero said gripping my shoulder and kissing me on the head.

I hadn't expected him to kiss me. As soon as he did, I scanned the room. Everyone was watching. I didn't know how to feel about it. But, it did feel good seeing how comfortable he was showing affection towards me. It filled a hole in my life that I didn't know I had.

With the Scrabble scores calculated and the person in second place declared champion, everyone else headed to bed.

"Did you want another drink?" Nero asked.

"I'm good. I'm still feeling the last one. But thank you," I told him with a smile.

The two of us looked at each other. When Nero didn't make a move, I did. Putting my hand on his thigh, I rubbed his leg.

"Did you want to head to bed?" I asked him.

"I guess."

"Hey, how did your mattress feel?"

"What do you mean?"

"I don't know. Mine was a little hard. Not bad or anything. I was just wondering how yours was."

Nero stared at me for a second.

"Did you wanna see?"

"I guess for comparison," I said unable to contain my smile.

"Then, let's go," Nero said getting up and taking my hand.

As we crossed the living room to the stairs, my heart thumped. There was no question what I wanted to happen next. I was in love with Nero. I wanted him to be my first. And approaching his bedroom, electricity danced across my skin with anticipation.

Flicking on the soft nightstand lights, we entered. Nero sat on the bed first.

"I don't know. It feels pretty good to me. What do you think?"

I sat next to him allowing our arms to brush against one another.

"It's nice," I said suddenly at a loss for words.

"You know I like you, right?" Nero said leaning even closer. "I've never met anyone like you. When I think of you, I think about forever. I said I was falling in love with you, but it's too late. I think I'm in love…"

That was when I kissed him. Throwing my legs around his waist I sat in his lap pushing my body against his. Wrapping my arms around his neck, I turned my attention to our kiss. Seeming thrown for a second, he quickly took control.

Pushing his fingers through my hair, he gripped and tugged. I loved it. Pressing his chest against mine, he parted our lips and pushed in his tongue. Finding mine, they danced. I lost myself in the sensation. Whipped away to another world all I could think about was our kiss. I wanted more. I wanted the two of us to become one.

Without thinking, I found myself grinding my open legs against his torso. I couldn't help it. The sensation felt too good. The mix of it and the kiss was a drug that I was immediately addicted to. So, when Nero reached down and stripped off my shirt, I did the same needing the full radiance of his body heat.

Shirtless, Nero scooped his arm under my ass and lifted me like it was nothing. Laying me onto the bed, he reached for the button on my pants. I untwined my legs letting him. With only my underwear left, he moved back up my body. Climbing on top of me, he glided his hands up my sides and onto my arms before pinning my hands on the bed above me.

Unable to resist, he stared at me knowing that I couldn't escape even if I wanted to. I didn't. I wanted to be exactly here. But, I wanted to get my hands on his body. And the fact that I couldn't, made me want him more.

Mercifully, Nero leaned down and kissed my lips. It was only for a second. He then kissed his way to my ear and my neck. Giving him full access, he then moved to my shoulder and then my chest.

When he got to my nipple, he bit it. The sensation sent shockwaves through me. It hurt but the pain felt good. I wanted him to stop as much as I wanted him to do it again.

When he released my hands and traveled lower, I reached for him and massaged his head. Without realizing it, I was pushing him further down. I couldn't forget how his lips had felt around my cock. It had been the greatest sexual experience of my life.

When his face got to my underwear, he rubbed his nose along my hard cock. Through the cloth, he took it into his mouth. The heat of it made my chest lift. When he finally pulled down my underwear and wrapped his large hands around my balls, I was twitching in desperate need of him.

Returning his lips to my tip, I ached for him. Taking my head into his mouth, I gripped the sheets. It was about then that he let go of my balls and rounded my ass.

Pushing into my cheeks, he found my hole. Massaging it, he lowered his mouth swallowing my cock. Everything he was doing was separating me from my body. I had to fight with everything I had to remain conscious.

Pressing my hole harder, I hoped I knew what would happen next. Releasing my cock, I heard him ask, "Yes?"

"Yes!" I moaned wanting him inside of me.

As if I had done something wrong, he let me go. The sudden loss of him caused me to open my eyes and look for him. On his knees, he was removing the last of his clothes. With his monster springing out, I couldn't take my eyes off of it.

I followed it as he climbed over me and reached for the nightstand. When Nero returned and squirted the contents of a bottle into his palm, I knew this was it.

Nero didn't disappoint. Slipping an arm under my knee, he rolled me onto my back. With my ass opening for him, he pushed his fingers onto my hole. His lube made it easier.

Applying pressure until his slick finger entered me, I yelped. Leaving it there until I relaxed around it, he gently removed it and worked his way on top of me.

With my ass rolling higher into the air, I stared up into Nero's beautiful blue eyes. I needed to kiss him. Again he didn't disappoint.

I could feel the tip of his cock look for my opening as our lips met. As I opened my mouth, his tip found my hole. Perching above me as I found his tongue, he thrust his hips until with intense pressure, he popped into me.

I moaned. He was so big. The pain that followed washed through me before settling like a crashed wave. Luckily, he didn't move as the feeling overwhelmed. But when it drained from me and I realized that the man I was in love with was in me, I pulled him tighter and began kissing him again.

Pushing deeper into me, my head danced. We were still kissing, but barely. Everything in me was focused on the sensation down below. With every moment, it was turning from pain to pleasure. And by the time he was legitimately fucking me, I knew why this was all some people talked about.

I had thought him sucking me was good, but there was no greater feeling than Nero's cock in my ass. He was in me. The two of us were one. I didn't ever want him to leave me. But as he fucked me harder and the pulse within me built, Nero's face twisted and I dug my fingers into his back.

"Ahhhh!" I groaned feeling the explosion crest.

My inner thighs tingled. My balls retracted trying to hold it back. But, when the ache and pressure got too much, I orgasmed with the force of a firehose.

I drenched our two chests. Nero didn't notice because he had an eruption of his own. Moaning like a feral animal, he filled me with everything he had. Buried in me, he couldn't stop flinching.

More than that, any move I made started the flinching again. It took forever for him to calm enough to cradle me in his arms. But, when he did, it was the greatest feeling in the world. He was still hard and inside of me and I loved it.

Eventually, he did lower my hips and slip out, but that was when he pulled a hand towel from the nightstand and cleaned us both off.

"What else do you have in there?" I joked about his nightstand.

"What do you need?"

"Wow, you came prepared. How confident were you?"

"I didn't know if it was gonna happen, but I hoped. And, it's better to have it and not need it…"

"Than to need it and not have it?"

"Exactly," he said with a smile.

With him pulling me back into his arms and rolling me on top of him, I rested my head on his chest.

"I think I'm starting to need you," I told him.

"Luckily, you have me."

Did I have him? I hoped I did. But I hadn't done anything like this before. I had never had a boyfriend. How did any of this work?

Although it took a while, eventually I fell asleep. I had good dreams. When I woke, we were in different positions, but he was still holding me. Wiggling so that my back could press against his chest, I realized that I had morning wood. Did he? Adjusting my hips, I learned he did.

Maybe I had done a little too much wiggling, or maybe just enough, but quickly I found the tip of his cock again pressed on my aching hole. I groaned and eased back onto him.

That was all I needed to do. Because for the second time in my life, and the last few hours, I felt a hard cock push into me and fill me up. Unlike the hard fucking that had happened last night, this time it was gentle and sensual. It didn't hurt going in and everything about it felt natural.

God, did I love this man. He was what I dreamed of. And when the thought of him became too much, I reached down and jerked my cock. That was when he sped up so that we could cum at the same time.

With a palm-full of my cum, I chuckled.

"I'm awake now," I told him.

"How's that for an alarm clock?"

"That's how I want to get up," I said with a smile.

"Every morning that you want it. I promise."

"I'll take you up on that," I said finally turning towards him and finding his lips.

After Nero pulled himself out of me and reached over retrieving another cloth from the nightstand, I cleaned myself off and turned to face him.

"I want to do something for you," I told him wanting to make him as happy as he had me.

"What's that?"

"I want to find out the situation around your birth father."

"I told you, you can try."

"Thanks. But, I don't think she'll open up to me if I just ask her. Do you know if she's going to the festival today?"

"She is. And, you don't know how much of a miracle that is. She hasn't done anything this social in about eight years."

"Wow! Huh! Do you think she would mind if I hung out with her today? If I had some alone time with her, she would probably feel more comfortable opening up."

"We could do that."

"No, I mean just me. I mean, you could if you want. She's your mother. But, I thought that if I have time with her without you, she might see me as someone she can share things with."

"Do you think it will work?"

"It's the best idea I've got. And, I promise you that I'll be able to tell you something you didn't know before. It may not be what I ask. But it will be something. Do you trust me to do that?"

"Yeah, I trust you," he said with a smile.

I leaned over and kissed him. I was excited to do this. It represented the very best I had to offer him.

Showering separately, Nero stayed in bed until I was done. I wanted to head downstairs first to start putting in time with his mother.

"Morning!" Everyone said looking like they had been up for hours.

"Morning. Are we late for breakfast?"

"A little. Where's Nero? I can scrabble a few more eggs to go along with the French toast I've cooked," Cage suggested.

"You made French Toast?" I turned to Quin. "How are you still so thin?"

"Believe me, it's all genetics," Quin said with a smile.

"Nero will probably be down in a few minutes. He was right behind me."

"I'll get started," Cage said going to work.

"Miss Roman, you must love having a son who cooks like this?" I asked the woman I sat next to.

"I just love having my son back. I don't care how he cooks," she said looking at Cage with joy.

I could tell that she wasn't going to be hard to get to know.

"Since I don't know anyone and Nero will be helping out with the festival, do you mind if I hang out with you today?" I asked her casually.

"It would be my pleasure," the dark-haired woman said wrapping my hand in hers.

Once Nero joined us, we sat around the table and planned our day. Most of the planning was Cage and Nero gently teasing Quin about the mascot costume he agreed to wear.

"Hey, I helped him make that thing," I said defending him.

"It was even his idea," Quin said.

"So, you're the one painting the target on my baby's back?" Cage asked amused.

"It's a moonshine festival! I thought he should be wearing a moonshine jug."

"And when drunk rednecks try to pop his cork and drink him, what are you gonna do then?" Nero asked playfully.

"Well, I thought the two of you did a wonderful job," Nero's mom said coming to our defense.

I grabbed her arm wrapping mine around hers. "Thank you, Miss Roman." I turned to the guys. "See. And you should always listen to your Mama."

Everyone laughed having a good time.

After Nero and I cleaned up, we packed up the trucks and headed to the festival. Nero's mom rode with us.

"Didn't you have to take care of that thing for Titus?" I asked him after we had been walking for a while.

"Oh right! It will probably take me, what?" He asked looking at me.

"Thirty? Forty-five minutes?" I suggested.

"Probably. You good with Kendall, Mama?"

"I'm just fine," she said crinkling the skin around her eyes with her smile.

With Nero gone, I asked her questions starting with the most basic ones possible. Hearing Nero's stories, I had an idea of what I should avoid. I think I succeeded and by the time Nero returned, she was telling me about where she grew up. It was in a nearby town. Somewhere fifty miles from here.

With Nero back, I switched up my questioning. I hinted at things that might be off-limits and danced around things that were probably too sensitive. But when I asked her what she had wanted to be when she grew up, I seemed to hit an unexpected nerve.

Tears filled her eyes as she explained.

"I wanted to be a ballerina."

"You wanted to be a dancer, Mama? I didn't know that about you?"

"Yep. I took classes and was very good. That's why you can dance around the field like you do. You got that from me."

"Not from his dad?" I asked casually.

She didn't respond. I was thinking she would ignore it completely, until she said, "He got his athletics from his dad. He got his dancing from me."

I didn't react because I was trying to keep her comfortable. But Nero couldn't help himself. He stared at her with his mouth hanging open.

"I got it from my dad?"

"That's what I said. Now, how about we try some of those moonshine muffins over there. Do you think they have alcohol in them?"

"Maybe. But what I really want to know is…"

I subtly put my hand on his forearm to silence him. He took my suggestion. Now that she unlocked the door, I knew I could get her to open it. But it was going to be a delicate operation. I was glad that Nero trusted me to execute it.

Purchasing a few of the muffins, we ate them as we caught up with Cage and Quin. Quin was walking around in his mascot costume posing for pictures with people while Cage attentively kept watch.

"It's quite the turnout," Cage said scanning the area. "Dr. Sonya should be pleased."

"Titus should be, too. He's all about these types of things," Nero said.

I turned to Quin. "You alright in there?"

"We didn't make armholes, or a hole to breathe through!"

"Oh yeah," I realized with a laugh. "Sorry, it was my first moonshine jug costume."

"I'm dying in here!"

"You can take it off whenever you want, ya know? I think you've done your duty," Cage told him.

"No, I can do it. I just need some water."

"Quin, why didn't you tell me that. Okay, I'm gonna get this one some water. What do you think? Pop the cork and pour it in?" Cage said with a smirk.

"It's not funny!" Quin exclaimed.

We all silently laughed. We had made eye holes but we had covered it with a fabric that made it hard to see through. I didn't think he would catch us.

"You know I can see you laughing, right? It's not funny!"

"That's right everyone," Cage said pretending he wasn't laughing too. "It's not funny. Quin is doing something very nice for the town. We should all thank him for it."

"Quin, you're doing a great job," Miss Roman said.

"Bang-up job," Nero told him.

"You are wearing that moonshine jug!" I said enthusiastically.

"Whatever. Cage, lead me away from here."

"You got it gorgeous," Cage said looking back at us with a playful glare.

"We're gonna have to make that up to him," Nero decided.

"Yeah. I'll invite him to dinner when we get back to school," I told him.

"I thought he looked quite nice," Nero's mother volunteered.

After a few more hours of food and moonshine shots, the sun began to set and Nero, his mother, and I headed home. Miss Roman was in a very good mood. Nero was too. So, when I suggested that we have drinks on the veranda, everyone agreed.

"When did you move here?" I asked her.

"A long time ago. I can barely remember it anymore."

"What brought you here?"

"I was pregnant with Nero," she said putting her hand on his forearm with a smile.

"I can't imagine raising a baby by myself. Did you know anyone here?"

"I didn't know a soul."

"Then, why here?"

"I don't know. I didn't want to move too far and I had always heard about this town."

"I didn't know anyone heard about this town," Nero snipped.

I held up my hand quieting him. I was getting a lot of answers so I didn't want him to accidentally change the mood. Seeing my gesture, he listened.

"That was one of the reasons I chose here, because the town wasn't well known."

"I hear a lot of people like small towns because it gives them a chance to be anonymous. Was that you?"

Her pleasant demeanor melted into deep thought. "That was one of the reasons."

I matched her mood. "Did it have to do with what happened to Cage? I can't imagine what it must be like to be told he had died when you knew he hadn't."

"It was very hard on me."

"How did you even function after something like that?"

"I didn't. Not for a long time."

"I guess it helps to have someone supporting you as you did."

"I didn't have anyone."

"What about Cage's father? He must have been there for you, wasn't he?"

"He didn't want me to have Cage in the first place."

"Oh no!"

"He was completely against it."

"But he knew you were pregnant?"

"Yeah."

"And you told him what happened at the hospital?"

"I told him. And the look he gave me afterward, told me all I needed to know."

"What do you mean? What did his look tell you?"

"That he had something to do with why I didn't have my baby," she said looking into my eyes with sadness.

"That's horrible! What do you think he did?"

"I don't know."

"Do you think he had Cage kidnapped?"

"I can't be sure. All I know was that it changed me. I couldn't get back to the person I was before and eventually, he didn't want to have anything to do with me. That's when I came up with a plan. I was going to get back what he took from me."

"What do you mean?" I asked.

"One day I asked to come by his place telling him if I did, I would leave him alone forever. He agreed.

When I got there, I made him his favorite drink and dropped something in it that I had gotten in Nashville. I had made a special trip there to find it," she said with a smile.

"What was it?"

"It was something that would help me to get what I deserved from him but he wouldn't remember."

"And, that's how I was born," Nero said realizing.

"That's how I got you," she said squeezing his forearms and staring into his eyes.

"You drugged him?"

Her tight-lipped smile dropped. She let him go and sat up.

"I did what I had to do to get back what he had taken from me," she said looking down.

"So, I'm only here because you…"

"Nero, do you mind getting me another drink," I said cutting him off.

He turned to me knowing what I was doing. I stared at him wide-eyed and shook my empty glass. He looked like he was about to ignore me when headlights lit the veranda. It was Cage and Quin pulling up.

"I'm feeling tired. It's been a long day. I hope you two don't mind if I head to bed early."

"Of course not. Do we, Nero?"

Nero met my unwavering glare and then relented.

"Of course not, Mama."

She got up. "Then tell Cage and Quin I said goodnight."

"We will," I told her before she went inside and disappeared for the night.

When she was gone, Nero turned to me and snapped.

"What did you do that for?"

"What did I do?"

"You kept shutting me up like that."

"You wanted answers, right? I was getting you your answers."

"The only answer I got was that I'm here because Mama raped some man."

"Shhh! Keep your voice down."

"Don't tell me to shut up. You heard her. She was mad because my dad took what she really wanted from her, so she drugged and raped him to get me. You heard her say it."

I was trying to think of some other way I could frame it, but my mind wasn't moving fast enough. He was right. That was what she had just explained. How do you make someone feel better once they learn that their existence is the result of rape?

"What are you two drinking?" Cage said standing in the doorway with a smile.

Nero looked at him with anger.

"What?"

Nero stared at him for a moment more then said, "Nothin'," and pushed past him headed inside.

"What just happened?" Cage asked me confused.

I wasn't sure how much to tell him. This had to do with him as much as it did Nero. But, was it my place to say anything? On the other hand, if he knew, maybe he could help Nero process it in a way I couldn't.

"Your mother just shared something about how Nero was born," I told him hesitantly.

"What?" He asked approaching me.

"I'm not sure if I should be the one to say."

"What's going on?" Quin said stepping outside and seeing the tension.

"Kendall said that Mama just told them something about how Nero was born."

"She told you two something about their father?"

"Not exactly," I said.

"Whatever it is, you have to tell us," Quin insisted. "This has been something Cage has been wondering about his whole life. You need to tell us, Kendall. There's no other choice you can make."

I still didn't know if I should, but I did. I told them what their mother had said to me and why.

"It was something I was hoping I could do for Nero. I thought knowing would help him. Now he's just... I don't know."

"You didn't know what she would say. Neither did I," Quin said.

"But you had a feeling he wouldn't like it?" I asked.

"I had a feeling."

"What do I do now?" I asked looking between them.

"Nero's been through a lot in his life. He'll figure out how to deal with this. I just wish it wasn't something that made him feel he wasn't wanted. He has enough of those."

"Yeah, he does," I confirmed remembering the horror stories he had told me. "So, what do I do tonight?"

The two of them looked at each other. They didn't have a clue. Neither did I. Did I give him his space? Did I climb into bed with him and offer him my body? I didn't know.

Not wanting to decide, I stayed on the veranda. Grabbing drinks, Cage and Quin joined me. The fun time everyone had had beforehand was gone. But we continued to talk.

Quin told me about his experience as the mascot and I told them a little more about myself. Even if I hadn't met Nero, I was pretty sure that I would have liked Quin and Cage. They were both great people. More than that, they were starting to feel like friends.

When they headed to bed, I did too. I wasn't going to return to the guest bedroom. Nero might have needed space, but I didn't want to create distance between us. I loved him. I wanted to be with him.

Allowing the light from the hallway to flood the room, I saw Nero already asleep in bed. At least, he looked asleep. Undressing, I joined him.

I would have been okay if he had wanted to use my body to feel better, but he didn't. The closest we got all night was when I couldn't take being apart from him anymore and I rolled over and touched his back. It was only then that I was able to fall asleep.

When I woke up the next morning, he was gone. The bed was empty. Getting dressed and going in search of him, I found him downstairs ready to leave. I was the last one down, so Quin and Nero were waiting on me.

"I'm sorry. You could have woken me," I explained.

"That's okay," Quin said. "My first class is this afternoon."

"Yours is at 8 AM, isn't it?" Nero asked.

"Oh, Jesus! Yeah. What time is it?" I asked.

"6:15," Nero said looking at me like we were strangers.

"Yeah, I guess we should go. Is your mother up? I should say goodbye."

"She doesn't usually get up until 7:30," Cage told me. "And, she had a few drinks yesterday, so she might decide to sleep in."

"Then I'll get my stuff."

I said goodbye to Cage letting him know how much fun I had had. And, driving back to campus, it was again Quin and I who did all of the talking.

"What building is your class in? I'll drop you there."

I told Nero and we pulled up in front of it. I was only ten minutes late.

"I had a lot of fun this weekend," I told Quin who sat in the backseat. "Thank you so much for inviting me."

"We're all really glad you came."

I looked over at Nero.

"This weekend was… nice!"

He didn't look at me.

"Yeah. I'll text you."

I wanted him to kiss me bye. He didn't. After being as affectionate as he had been all weekend, it couldn't be because Quin was there. It had to be what he had learned about his birth. He was clearly having a hard time dealing with it.

"Okay," I told him before collecting my travel bag, getting out of the truck, and watching him drive away.

As much as I wanted to stand there thinking about what I should do next with Nero, I knew I had to get to class. Entering as quietly as I could, I found a seat in the back and pulled out my phone to take notes. When the class ended, my plan was to sneak out.

"Kendall, can I speak to you for a moment?" Professor Nandan said as I tried.

As large as the class was, I didn't think he would notice that I was late. I was readying my excuse when he brought up something else.

"How's your experience with Nero, going?"

Oh, of course he was asking me about my time with Nero. The student counselor program is what he had been working on his whole career.

"I think it's going well. In fact, that's why I was late. He had invited me to the town where he grew up so I could get better insight into the origins of his issues."

"He invited you to go home with him?"

"Yeah. There was also a festival this weekend. I had helped his brother's boyfriend build a costume for it so he was the one who actually invited me. I mean, they both did. But, I went because of Quin."

"Quin?"

"His brother's boyfriend. He has a house there. They moved into it this weekend." I thought about it and laughed. "I guess there was a lot going on."

Professor Nandan stared at me suspiciously.

"What?"

"It's my mistake for not saying this before, but dating someone you're trying to help is never a good idea."

"Dating?" I said feeling my face flush. "No! Why would you suggest that?"

"It's okay if you are dating him. I don't want to make it seem like there would be anything wrong with it. But, if you are, I will have to assign someone else as his counselor."

"Why?"

"Trust and consistency are the two bedrocks to counseling. It is often what allows people to open up and work through their feelings."

"I'm both of those things."

"And, that's great. But, the complexity introduced by intimate relationships often interrupts that. Again, there's nothing wrong if you two are dating. It would mean you've made progress with your bias against football players. But, as a person trusted with Nero's mental health, I would be required to remove you from your role with him."

I looked at my professor not knowing what to say but knowing I had to say something soon. Weren't Nero and I dating? Hadn't we had sex? Hadn't he told me he loved me? Didn't I love him?

At the same time, I didn't want anyone else to be assigned to him. He was making tremendous progress with me as his counselor. He had opened up so much. And hadn't I gotten the answer to a question he had wondered about his whole life?

Sure, we might have experienced a bump in the road as he's processing it. But, I was the one who had done that for him. No one else could have. I'm the only one who could help him in the way he needs it. I'm positive about that.

"Don't worry, Professor Nandan. The two of us are just counselor and counseled," I said with a forced smile. "And, I think he's making a lot of headway. He's opened up a lot. I think I'm helping him."

Professor Nandan looked at me skeptically but relented. "Well, I'm glad to hear that. His coach did mention that he's been playing better than ever."

"See. I've been helping him. You can trust me, Professor Nandan. I have his best interest at heart."

"That's good to hear," he said finally relaxing. "But, keep in mind that your counseling doesn't give you permission to be late for my class."

"I'm sorry about that. It'll never happen again. Or, at least, I'll try," I said with a smile.

"You do that," he said smiling back.

As sure as I was that I was the one who could best help Nero, my professor's words did linger as I walked back to my room. I knew the rule against dating someone you're helping. Everyone does. I never thought I would have to worry about it because I never thought I would date anyone much less a client.

Yet, here I was sleeping with the first person whose mental health I had been entrusted with. What did that say about me?

I would like to think that this was a special circumstance. After all, I did kiss him before he had been assigned to me. We had established our attraction for each other before our work together began.

Besides, wasn't it Nero's attraction to me that got him to open up? Would he have come out to a complete stranger? He certainly wouldn't have invited them to his place for the weekend. And, if they weren't in his hometown, Nero couldn't take them to the lake and share his painful story.

No, it was a good thing that the two of us had the relationship we did. It was helping him. But, as his counselor, maybe it was better if I slowed things down. I wanted to be his boyfriend. I wanted to rush to his side and wrap my arms around him until he felt better. However, a good counselor would give him the time and space he needed to process it all.

He said that he would text me. So, instead of pushing him, I would wait for his text. It would be what a typical therapist would have to do. And, it wasn't like I needed to hear from him every day. It wasn't like I needed him to breathe or anything... Evan Carter!

Prickles shot through my body like jagged rocks. I whipped around replaying the image in my mind. I saw Evan Carter. It took me a moment to realize it but I had. At least I thought I had. I thought I had seen him standing in the quad staring at me.

I didn't see him now. Scanning everywhere, I didn't even see someone trying to hide or get away. Had it just been in my head? Double-checking my surroundings, I considered that it could have been.

Thinking I had seen Evan when I hadn't wasn't a new thing. It used to happen a lot, especially my freshman year. I used to think I saw him everywhere. He was the boogeyman sitting in my periphery. Whenever I looked for him, though, he was never there.

But all that had stopped. I had barely thought about him after Nero beat the shit out of him. I had gotten my justice. What Nero had done had allowed me to move on.

Re-centering myself, I took a deep breath and continued to my room. I reminded myself that I didn't have to be scared of Evan Carter anymore. Nero had taken care of it for me. Nero had put the fear of God in him. There was no way he would dare show his face here even if he knew where I was. But, I was sure that he didn't. And I knew Nero would keep me safe… that is if we were still together.

Initially, I thought questioning how Nero felt about me was me being insecure. After all, we had spent the weekend together opening up about the most intimate parts of our lives and having sex. No one could go cold that quickly.

But, as the days passed and I hadn't heard from him, I began to wonder. Could I really mean so little to him that he could disappear for days without a word?

Sure, he was dealing with some heavy stuff about how he was born, but didn't he love me? Why didn't he want to share what he was thinking with me?

"What are you doing?" Cory asked me as I stared at my phone.

"I'm trying to make my phone ring with my mind," I explained.

"That's what I thought you were doing. You know that you could just text him, right?"

"I can't."

"Why not?"

"Because he said he would text me."

"So, that means you can't text him?"

"Kind of."

"And, you've determined this how?"

"I don't know. Isn't that what you're supposed to do?"

"Is there a rule book somewhere I didn't see?" Cory joked.

"Isn't there?"

"Huh!" Cory said getting into bed.

"What?"

"I thought a relationship between two guys would be different."

"What do you mean?"

"I guess I thought that it was only with a guy and girl that someone wished the other person would text instead of just texting."

"Are you saying that I'm the girl in this relationship, or whatever is going on between Nero and me?"

Cory sat up defensively. "I did not say that! Your words. Not mine." He paused. "But, now that you've said it, aren't you kinda acting that way?"

I didn't know how to respond. I didn't find it insulting that he was implying I was the girl and I didn't think Cory meant it to be. But, what he was also implying was that I wasn't being active in the creation of my life. That didn't sit well with me.

The reason I had gotten my ass kicked so much in high school was because I wouldn't conform to what others thought I should be. When they tried to put me in a box, I broke the box. I was an active participant in my life. I didn't like Cory suggesting I was being passive.

"You're right! If I want to talk to him, I should just text him. I don't know why I was waiting."

I stared at my phone.

"Then why aren't you texting him?"

"Give me a second."

I could feel Cory's hot gaze on me as I sat there.

"You're still not texting him."

"Alright! I'll text him. I just need to figure out what to say."

"'Hi?' 'Hello?' 'Why haven't you texted me all week you inconsiderate asshole?' Those are all good options."

I stared at Cory surprised. "You should not be more upset about this than I am."

"It just that you said things happened between you two last weekend and then he ghosted you. That's bullshit!"

"First of all, he didn't ghost me. At least, I don't think he did. And, second of all, he's got stuff going on."

"You've got stuff going on. Hasn't he thought about that? You deserve to be happy too, ya know."

As grateful as I was for Cory's righteous anger, I had to wonder where it was coming from.

"Is everything alright, Cory?"

"What do you mean?"

"You seem… animated tonight. Is everything good between you and Kelly?"

"It's just that she never says what she wants. It's like I'm supposed to read her mind or something. Everything's a guessing game with her. It's so tiring! I just wish she would say what she wants instead of getting upset when she doesn't get the thing she never told me she wanted… ya know?"

"Okay, I'll text Nero! See, I'm texting him," I said exaggerating my typing while reading aloud. "Hey Nero, long time no hear from. Did you want to get together to talk about what happened?" I pressed the button. "See, I sent it. It's done. I'm not trying to get him to read my mind…"

I stopped when my phone dinged.

"Is that him?" Cory asked.

"Yeah."

Cory sat next to me on my bed and looked at my screen as I read it.

"He says he's flying out for an away game tomorrow morning."

"Did you know he had an away game this weekend?"

"No."

"Ask him if he wants to get together tonight," Cory suggested.

I looked at Cory to figure out what was going on. "You are awfully invested in this."

"What? I just want to see you happy. Text it."

I did what he said and quickly got a reply.

"Can't. Getting up early," I read. "What do I text now?" I asked with a hint of snark.

Cory leaned back deep in thought. He really was invested in this more than I was. I wasn't sure what it was, but something was going on with Cory.

"Maybe you wish him luck on the game and ask if you could get together when he gets back?"

I shrugged and typed it figuring it was as good of a reply as any.

"Sent."

'Ok,' was what followed.

Cory returned to his bed looking more nervous than I was. It felt like he was living vicariously through me. What was up with that?

I certainly appreciated not going through this alone. But, he was a happily married man, or something close to it. Why would he want to vicariously live my gay relationship?

I set that mystery aside and returned my thoughts to Nero. He had replied to my texts very quickly. It didn't seem like he was playing games. Then, why hadn't I heard from him? Had he just been waiting for me to reach out?

Knowing that I needed a fix of Nero one way or another, I sent a text to Quin.

'Are you around this weekend?'

He didn't reply as quickly as Nero, but I didn't have to wait long to hear back from him.

'I have to work this weekend, so I'll be around.'

'Dinner Saturday night?'

'Sure.'

I would have preferred to have Nero, but Quin was a great consolation prize. I liked spending time with Quin. He was the first guy I felt I had a lot in common with.

Cory was great and had been a lifesaver over the years. But, he was also straight and in a relationship with his girlfriend since birth. As a gay guy who only recently lost his virginity, there weren't too many areas we could connect on.

Looking forward to our dinner almost as much as a date, I was excited when our meeting time rolled around. Frankly, I was also a little nervous. If it wasn't for Nero and the fact that Quin wasn't my physical type, I would think I was developing a crush on him.

"This is a nice place," I told him when we arrived at the Italian restaurant.

"It was one of the first places I went with Lou… and Cage."

"I don't think I've met Lou."

"He's my roommate."

"I know. Nero's mentioned him."

"Really?" Quin asked confused.

"He came up in a conversation about Titus."

"About Titus?"

"Yeah. Aren't they dating or something?"

Quin laughed. "Why would you think they're dating?"

His reaction surprised me. "I don't know. Maybe it was something that Nero said."

"I think they're just friends."

"Okay. I would still like to meet him sometime."

"Maybe I'll book a slot in his schedule for a game night. That is, as long as you and Nero are free."

"Sounds good. By the way, have you heard from Nero?"

"From Nero? Not really. He doesn't reach out to me like that."

"Oh! He's not a texter?"

"He's pretty good at replying. But, I don't think I've ever gotten a text from him asking me how I was doing."

"That sounds like him," I said feeling relieved.

"By the way, how are things going with him? You two seemed snuggly last weekend."

"I thought things were going great. But then his mom said what she did and now he's M.I.A."

"I wouldn't worry about it. He can get like that. If you give him a few days, I'm sure things will settle," Quin said as he pulled his phone out of his pocket.

Flicking the screen on, Quin squinted as he read a text. With a few more swipes I heard the audio from a video. As soon as someone woohoo'd he lowered the volume. Continuing to watch, Quin looked more uncomfortable.

"What is it?"

Quin opened his mouth to speak then stopped and watched the video to the end.

"You're freakin' me out a little, Quin. What's going on?"

Quin looked up at me rattled.

Cage just sent me a video that his old teammate posted on one of his socials.

"What was the video?"

"Umm," Quin's eyes bounced around.

"Seriously, Quin. You're freakin' me out."

"Sorry. Maybe you should just watch it."

Quin handed me his phone. The first frame of the video filled the screen. It was of Nero. He had a woman dancing on his lap and she was butt-ass naked.

I looked up at Quin who was stone-faced. Returning to the phone I pressed play. I couldn't tell if he was in a strip club or somewhere else. But there were other football player-looking guys standing around watching as Nero motor-boated the naked woman's huge breasts.

What was most upsetting was that he seemed to love it. He stared at her body wide-eyed. When she moved her naked hips to grind inches from his face, his head dipped in as if he wanted to take her into his mouth. It was as he dipped forward a second time that the video cut off.

"I'm sorry," Quin said looking at me heartbroken.

I didn't know what to say or think. Was this what he did every time his team took a road trip? Was someone like her who he really wanted? Had I been a fool to fall for Nero?

Once again a football player had hurt me. It might not have been in the way it was in high school, but it hurt just as much. Maybe more.

"Kendall, I don't think this is Nero."

"You don't think that's him in the video?"

"No, it's him. But, I don't see him choosing to do something like that."

"Yet, there he is doing it. Where did you say Cage found it?"

"I think it was on an ex-teammate's Instagram account."

"So, everyone has seen this?"

"Not everyone. I'm sure it's just a few people. I'm going to ask Cage to ask his teammate to take it down."

As Quin texted, I thought about what I had just seen. Hadn't Nero talked about wanting to go pro? Why would he put himself in this situation?

"Do you think Nero knows the video was posted?" I asked Quin.

"I don't know. Cage didn't say whether he sent it to him."

"I'll text him about it," I said curious about what Nero would say.

After I hit 'send,' I waited for a response. If nothing else, Nero was always a fast responder. But this time, nothing.

I stared at the phone waiting for it. When it became clear that nothing was coming, I placed my phone beside my plate face up.

It was possible that whatever was developing between Nero and me was over. Maybe this was his way of telling me. It would be an insanely self-destructive way. But, if he wasn't in a good place, he could do anything.

"Cage sent the video to Nero. I told him to let me know if he hears back from him."

Quin and I continued to eat dinner but the night was clearly ruined. It felt like neither of us had anything to say. If things were over between Nero and me, didn't that mean that Nero would take Quin with him? They were practically family. Who was I past a guy Nero had sex with?

When dinner was over I reached for the check to split it and Quin insisted on paying. I let him. Nero had told me Quin's background and I had spent the weekend in his home. If he wanted to treat me to dinner, I was fine with it.

"So, I'll see you soon?" I asked him as we stood in front of the restaurant.

"Yeah. We should do this again."

"Absolutely. Whatever weekend you're not heading up to Snow Tip Falls."

"Sure," Quin said with a smile.

I wanted to hug him, but I didn't think he was a hugging sort of guy. I wasn't sure I was either. So, instead, we went our separate ways and I walked home.

Crossing back onto campus I checked my phone. Nero still hadn't replied. Was it because he was on a plane? Was he just ignoring me?

The worst version of every scenario raced through my mind when I suddenly spun around. With the door to my dorm room feet in front of me, I thought I saw someone in my periphery. Evan Carter. I had been distracted, but thinking back on the last ten minutes, I remembered the feeling that someone had been following me.

With my heart racing, I checked the shadows. Was I just being paranoid? Why would he be here? Hadn't Nero made clear what would happen if he ever came looking for me? And, with Nero slipping out of my life, what protection would I have if it was Evan?

Not finding anyone, I jogged to my building never taking my eyes off of the darkness behind me. When I was safely inside, I peered through the small glass in the door searching for him. Nothing moved.

Maybe I was going insane. Had the shaky connection between Nero and me triggered something? I thought I was over this? I thought I had worked past my Evan Carter nightmares.

"You okay?" Cory asked when I entered our dorm room.

"I don't know."

"What's going on?" He said giving me his full attention.

I wasn't sure what I should tell him.

"There's a video of Nero getting a lap dance at a strip club."

"Was the stripper a man or a woman?"

"It was a woman."

"Oh!"

"Why did you say it like that?"

"I don't know. You said he was into girls too, right?"

"I think so."

"Huh," he said getting lost in thought.

"Are you suggesting that because he's bisexual this should be expected?"

Cory looked at me shocked. "Why, is that a thing?"

"It's a stereotype."

"I didn't know that."

"Why would you, Mister I'm-A-Boring-Straight-Guy?"

Cory looked at me hurt. I didn't know why?

"Sorry. You're not boring. I'm just... I don't know what I am."

"You're scared you're gonna lose the guy you like," Cory said with empathy.

His words pierced my heart spilling its contents onto the floor between us.

"I am," I admitted slowly melting into tears. "What is it about me that no one can love?"

Cory put his arms around me gripping me tightly. I put my head on his shoulder. As heartbroken as I was, I knew how lucky I was to have Cory. If only he was into guys… and not practically married.

Cory didn't let me go the entire night. We slept like that and it did help. When we both woke up, it was a little awkward. It probably had to do with the both of us having morning wood. I had been the little spoon so it didn't matter. But with him pulling me onto him, I was sure I felt something. What made it weirder was how little he did to hide it.

What was going on with Cory? I had always dismissed the things he said over the years as signs he rejected toxic masculinity. But was I missing the forest through the trees?

I knew I shouldn't have done this considering how kind he was being to me, but as we laid there, I slowly pushed my hips back. I wanted to see if he was really spooning me with an erection.

It didn't take me long to find it. Cory wasn't small. And as soon as I made clear contact with it, he pulled away and quickly left my bed.

"Sorry," he said unable to look me in the eyes.

What was going on with him? I watched as he collected his towel and bath supplies and scurried towards the door.

"Should we talk about…"

"No!" He said startling me.

Realizing how harsh he had said it, he calmed himself.

"I told Kelly I would meet up with her for breakfast. I gotta go," he told me before exiting for the showers.

Figuring out what was going on with Cory was a good distraction. But eventually, my mind turned back to what was going on with Nero. Picking up my phone, I still didn't find a reply. He wasn't going to text me back. What we had had really was over. I had no idea what had gone wrong between us. My chest ached thinking about it.

Getting out of bed to get breakfast, I went through my day like a zombie. I didn't understand. It was just a week ago that I was lying in Nero's arms. Why had this happened?

Mercifully, the day eventually ended and I fell asleep. I was not looking forward to seeing Professor Nandan for my 8 AM class. Trying to hide in back, there was a moment when our eyes connected. Crap! He had seen me.

"Please reference your syllabus for this week's reading. And, Kendall, can I see you before you go?" The professor said collecting his notes and packing his bag.

I did not want to speak to him. Last week he had warned me about mixing counseling with relationships. It didn't even take a week for him to be proven right. I thought I had it all under control. But now Nero wasn't even texting me back. Everything was a mess.

"There's a video with Nero circulating online. Have you seen it?"

"What?"

"I think it's from the away trip he just took. Anyway, it's become a national story."

"Really? Why?"

"Because Nero is considered to be the best draft prospect at his position. ESPN has been keeping an eye on him for a while. So, when they found the video, it gave them something to talk about."

"I… I didn't know."

"You haven't spoken to him recently?"

"The last time was on Thursday."

"Huh. Well, to do a little damage control on Nero's career, the university's public relations team has set up an interview with a news outlet. Considering you're his student counselor, I thought it would be good if you were there."

"Me?"

"Yeah. Would you be okay with that?"

I considered it. As I did, it became clear why separating emotions and therapy was so important. I hurt thinking about how big of a mistake I had made.

Now the question was, would I admit to my professor that Nero and I had had sex so he could replace me and I could fight for our relationship? Or, would I prove to myself that I could be a professional by pushing my feelings for Nero aside and being there for him like I was supposed to be?

Chapter 10

Nero

Everything was spinning. It was like life had become a merry-go-round. I wasn't meant to have been born. My mother had drugged whoever the unlucky man was and had raped him. And she had done it because she had lost the son she really wanted. Where did that leave me?

I was a mistake. I should never have existed. How was I supposed to live knowing the world would be better off if I wasn't here?

Ever since I had learned the truth from my mother, things around me became more and more hazy. It was like I was losing control of the steering wheel of my life. I hadn't meant to let Kendall slip away, but I had. I hadn't wanted to go to a New Orleans strip club, but I went. And I certainly didn't want a lap dance, but my teammates pushed her on me so I acted like they expected me to.

Now everyone's pissed. Cage is texting me about it. Coach is telling me that I might not get drafted because of it. And, I'm pretty sure I've lost my boyfriend.

I'm not 100% on that because I still hadn't replied to him sending me the video. I couldn't handle knowing that the only guy I've ever loved hated me. There was a limit to how much I could take.

"Are you ready to do this?" Coach asked when he joined me in his office.

"Yeah. Whatever."

He paused and stared down at me on the couch.

"Do you not want to be here? Because, let me remind you that we're only here to salvage your professional career. But if you don't give a shit about it, then we could tell everyone to go home and be done with it right now."

"No. I wanna do this. I just… It's not fair."

"What's not fair? That everyone is bending over backward to save your reputation? Well, sometimes life isn't fair."

"But, I didn't want the lap dance. I didn't ask for it."

"And if you acted like that in the video, then we wouldn't be here. Look, what's happened has happened. Do you wanna deal with it head-on, or let the millions of people who now only know you as the strip club guy on East Tennessee's football team, define how the rest of your life goes? You wanna take charge of your future, or let your past dictate what happens next?"

I thought about that. Yeah, my life was spinning out of control and not for the first time. But, even when I was a kid, the one thing I knew I could count on was football. I was good at it. And it didn't matter what my mother was doing or not doing. It didn't matter how lonely I felt.

All that ever mattered was how well I could catch a pass and how fast I could get down the field. The rest of my life faded into the background when that was happening. Football was the only thing that had always been there for me. If I were going to fight for anything, it had to be that.

"I wanna take charge of my future."

"Good. Because you could have a bright one. It was a tragedy what happened to your brother. I can't help but think of his draft-ending injury as my fault somehow. I didn't want to let you down too," he said putting his hand on my shoulder.

"Thanks, Coach," I said meaning it.

"Now. I'm gonna need to ask you a personal question. Are you dating anyone?"

"What does that matter?" I asked feeling my skin flush as I thought about Kendall.

"Because what you did isn't illegal. You're young. You're an alpha male. Right or wrong, people will accept if you were just following your impulses. So, if you told the world that you're single, and subtly reminded them that you didn't violate any moral code, they'll forgive you.

"Yeah, some people are always looking to feel superior, so not everyone will give you a pass. But, if you say it in the right way, the 'Boys will be boys' narrative could take hold. So, I'm asking you, Nero, are you single right now?"

I sat listening to everything he had to say. If I understood him right, he was saying that life was fucked up. 'Boys will be boys'? What type of shit was that?

But, it wasn't like I ever believed that life was fair. I was turned into the worst person I could think of to survive. Was that fair? So, if this was the break I got in exchange for my messed-up childhood, I was gonna take it.

"There's nobody," I told him sure it was true.

Even if there was a chance that Kendall didn't hate me, it wasn't like he would want to be with me again. I was a fucked up piece of shit mess. I wouldn't want to be with me if I could help it. So there was no way a guy as great as Kendall would.

"Good. So, in the interview, I want you to focus on that. Say that it was innocent fun blowing off steam after a game and that as a single guy, you hadn't meant it to hurt or embarrass anyone. But, really hit the fact that you're single. And be as humble as you can be. Can you do that?"

"Yeah."

"I'm serious, Roman. This is important. Not just for you but for the football program. Can you do that?"

"Yes, sir. I can do it," I said steeling my heart to what saying those words meant.

"Good," he said again squeezing my shoulder, but this time with a smile. "You're gonna do a great job out there. The interview is with the Nashville channel 5's sports reporter. But, we expect it to go viral. So, try to be relaxed, but don't forget that millions will be watching."

"So, act like I'm on the field?"

Coach smiled. "You got this. Come on," he said ushering me out of his office towards an improvised media room. "By the way, the guy in charge of that program you're in for your temper insisted that I invite your student counselor. So, he'll be there too."

"Kendall?" I asked as a bolt of pain shot through me.

"Is that his name?" Coach asked before opening a door and ushering me through.

In a full panic, I scanned the room. There he was standing next to the guy behind the camera. When our eyes met, I saw his pain. Had I done that to him? I'm sure I had. Everything in me wanted to rush over and throw my arms around him. I couldn't. And when I didn't, his gaze fell to the floor.

"You ready, Nero?" Coach asked me pointing me in front of a large green screen. "Nero!"

"Yeah, I'm ready," I said slowly remembering what I had to do.

I didn't know what it meant that Kendall was here. Maybe he was forced to be here like I was. I couldn't let him distract me, though. His presence didn't mean anything. Football was still the only thing I could count on in my life and I was going to do whatever I had to to hold onto it.

The guy behind the camera approached me and gave me an earpiece.

"On the other end of that is a producer at the station. He'll give you a countdown to when you go live with Jill Walsh."

"The sports reporter's a woman?" I asked turning to Coach wondering how it was going to change things. He nodded encouragingly.

"You know they have those now?" the cameraman said before returning next to Kendall.

Of course I knew there were female sports reporters, I wanted to yell. I wasn't a stupid thug. I was tired of dealing with the way everyone saw me. I couldn't take it anymore. I was going to show them.

"You there? You ready?" the guy in the earpiece asked.

"I'm here. I'm ready."

"Standing by. We're going live in five, four, three, two…"

"Tonight we have a special interview with Nero Roman the East Tennessee football player in the center of a far-reaching scandal. Nero, thank you for joining us."

"It's my pleasure to talk to you. I just wish it was under more pleasant circumstances like a game-winning play."

"And, just to let the audience know, you've had a lot of those, the most of any freshman in Tennessee state history."

"I didn't know that," I said sincerely. "I just play the game the best I can. If I'm blessed with stats like that, then it's thanks to the teammates I've been lucky to play with."

"So, you seem like you have your life together. How did you end up in the middle of a scandal like this?"

"I honestly don't know. After the game, someone suggested that we go out. One thing led to another and I guess one of my teammates recorded it."

"And posted it online."

"And posted it. But, I'd like to point out that, we were just blowing off steam. It wasn't like I was cheating on anyone. There's no one. I'm single. We were just having a little fun."

"So, this is a case of boys being boys?" She suggested to my surprise.

"I guess. Though, I can now see how I was showing poor judgment. I deeply regret the embarrassment I brought to the East Tennessee Football program and the school's community. If I regain the trust of everyone around me, I think I could make everyone proud," I said speaking out of my ass.

"I'm sure you will. As for East Tennessee's perfect record so far this season?"

"We're gonna do everything we can to maintain it and bring another national championship to East Tennessee."

"There you have it. The sincere words of a present and future star in Tennessee football."

"And, we're clear," the producer said returning to the earpiece. "Great interview. Even I believed you. Good luck for the rest of the season."

"Thank you," I told him before handing the earpiece back to the cameraman whose inner asshole had softened.

"Roman, that was fantastic! I didn't know you had it in you," Coach said with a smile. "You are gonna go far in this world. Very far!"

I smiled and subtly looked around for Kendall. He looked as devastated as I thought he would be. Looking like he would burst into tears, he rushed out of the room.

I didn't go after him. Why not? I don't know.

With the coach releasing me, he told me to stay out of trouble at least until the interview airs. He said it in a way that made it sound like it would be hard for me. I didn't know what to think about that. Luckily, there were other things on my mind. Mostly it was Kendall and what I had let slip through my fingers.

The closer I got to my room, the more rage I felt towards myself. I was such an incredible fuckup. Everything about my life was a shit show, probably because I was the mistake who never should have been born.

By the time I had made it back to my place, I was ready to explode. I tried to think of something that would calm me, but the one person who centered me was the reason I was so furious. Unable to hold it in anymore, I grabbed my heavy wooden bed frame and flipped it. It slammed into the wall with a crash.

Nothing I owned was safe after that. Anything I had that could break, I smashed against the wall. Anything that could tear, I tore apart. The place was a mess with torn paper and shattered glass when I ran out of stuff. That was when I looked across the room and marched towards Titus's side.

It was at that moment that the door unlocked and Titus stepped in. He scanned the room in shock. Seeing how out of control I was, he rushed to me.

Unsure what he would do, I reacted. With a flashback to every fight I had been in, I turned my body and caught him in the jaw. He hit the ground with one blow.

I froze catching myself. What had I done? He wasn't moving.

"Titus?" I said scrambling to his side. "Are you okay?"

His body lay lifeless. Had I knocked him out? Had I finally killed somebody? Was this the moment I had always been afraid would happen? It had to be.

With him still limp, I rushed to my feet, collected my keys, and escaped. I was trying not to run. It would make things too obvious. But I needed to get away. I needed to get to my truck and drive until I couldn't go any further.

Maybe I would drive to the lake I ran to as a kid and this time cross it. Maybe I would drive into it and bring my miserable life to an end.

I wasn't meant to be here. I wasn't meant to be alive. And the only question now was if I would have the courage to put an end to the mistake my mother had made so long ago.

Chapter 11

Kendall

I ran out of the media room leaving Nero behind. I couldn't believe he had said that. Had I meant nothing to him? I thought I had. Didn't he say he loved me?

I could only hold back my tears until I was outside running back to campus. With no one around, I bawled. I had been such a fool. I was an idiot to think that someone like him could love me. And it was a mistake to give a football player a chance.

They were all the same. Perhaps Nero had found a different way to hurt me. But, in every way, this was worse. At least I had my protective barrier around me in high school. Nero had gotten me to bare my heart. With it exposed, he had reached in and ripped it from my chest.

As the thoughts overwhelmed me, I slowed looking for a place to collect myself. Looking around, I realized where I was. This was where Nero and I had escaped to after I panicked realizing who I had been assigned.

I found the bench we had chosen and sat down. The tears didn't stop. With my elbow on my knees, I cried into my hands. I had tried to push my feelings for him aside and be a professional, but how could he be so cruel? Didn't he have a heart? Hadn't he cared about me at all?

"Kendall, are you okay?"

It took a second for the words to register. Someone was standing in front of me. They were in arm's reach and the voice sounded familiar. It took me a moment to place it, but when I did, terror tore through me like a fireball. Evan Carter.

I looked up finding the vision from my nightmares staring back at me. This was it. He was going to kill me for what Nero did to him. I needed to get away.

"Leave me alone!" I said jumping up and backing off.

"No, wait. I'm not here to hurt you. I just wanna talk," he said holding up his hands.

"Sure you are. Just like in high school. What are you gonna do this time, beat me to an inch of my life and leave me for dead?"

"Jesus, no! Fuck! Why would you say that?"

"Why would I say that?" I asked shocked. "Have you forgotten all of the things you did to me? Because I haven't. I still dream about them. I can't get them out of my head."

Horror flashed across Evan's face hearing my words. He was stunned. Stopping his pursuit, he yelled, "I'm sorry! I'm so sorry," he said before falling to his knees overwhelmed.

Wait, what?

I didn't understand what was going on. It startled me so much that I slowed to a stop. Had he just apologized to me? He did. And it sounded like he meant it.

I stood staring at him wondering what I should do. I could walk away, but Evan had just given me what I had dreamed about for so long. And he had without a threat to his life.

"I was such an asshole to you. And I know what you're thinking. You're thinking that I'm only here because you broke into my house with that guy and now I regret what happened. But no. I've always regretted it. There hasn't been a second I haven't hated myself for doing those things to you."

Now I was really confused.

"I don't understand. If you regretted doing them, then why did you?"

Evan looked up. There were tears in his eyes. Actual tears. I didn't think he was capable of human emotions.

"You have to have known. Out of everyone, you had to know. There's no way you didn't."

"I hate to tell you this, but I don't know what the hell you're talking about," I said approaching him.

"Don't you remember when it all started?"

I searched my memory.

"When what started? You were always a dick to me. You were an asshole from the first time we met."

"That's not true. You have to know that's not true."

"I don't. Because it is," I said defiantly.

"Freshman year we were in the same art class. Remember?"

I thought back.

"Mr. Adderley."

"Yeah."

"So?"

Evan flinched painfully. It confused me even more.

"I didn't know who I was back then. I hadn't joined the football team yet. I was still trying to figure things out. But, I knew that when I first saw you, I felt different. I couldn't explain it because I had no words for it. All I knew was that I wanted to talk to you.

"So, after a few weeks of losing my nerve, I built up my courage and approached you."

"You said you liked my art," I suddenly remembered.

"Right."

"And I responded by… shitting on you," I admitted.

"You didn't say thank you or start talking to me. You told me it was what talent looked like and I would know that if I had any."

"Right."

"Why would you say that? I was trying to be friends with you. I liked you."

"You liked me?"

"Yeah, Kendall. I liked you. I liked you a lot. There was a long time when I couldn't stop thinking about you."

The realization of what Evan was telling me flicked on like a light. As soon as it did, everything that happened made sense. Almost everything.

"So, you're what? Gay?"

Evan lowered his head.

"Then, why would you make my life hell. I was the only out gay guy in the school!"

"Because you were the only out gay guy in the school. Kendall, you did make me accepting who I was easy."

I looked at him stunned. "I didn't make your self-acceptance easy? I don't even know where to begin with that. You made everything about my self-acceptance the hardest thing in the world."

"I know. And I'm so sorry about that. But, please, see it from my perspective."

I stared at him pissed. "Which is?"

"You were the only gay guy that anyone at our school knew about. So, anyone who hinted that they might like guys would immediately be compared to you."

"And?"

"Did you have to wear dresses to school? Did you have to wear makeup?"

"Yes, I did. Because people like you were telling me that I couldn't. I had to prove that I wasn't going to give in to your bullshit. I wasn't gonna be ashamed of myself."

Evan lowered his head. "I get it. It just didn't make things easy for me. That's all. I didn't want to wear dresses. I didn't want to wear makeup. I just liked guys. So, since you were the only gay guy I'd ever met…"

"You thought there was only one way to be gay," I suddenly realized. "So you hated yourself because who you felt like didn't match what you thought you had to be."

"Exactly!" Evan said excitedly.

I looked at him blankly. Lifting my hands, palms open in front of me, I slowly turned them until my fingertips were pointed at me.

"What?"

I emphasized that my fingers were pointed at me.

"I don't get it."

"Evan, that's what I was going through. Do you think I had it any easier than you did?"

"You didn't? How could you not? Your parents had to have accepted who you were."

"Tolerating it isn't the same thing as accepting it. Why do you think I kept doing the things I did? I was trying to create a space large enough for me to be myself without people looking at me strangely for it. That's why I wore dresses and makeup, so that whatever else I did, it wouldn't compare."

"I get that now," Evan said nodding his head. "But, that doesn't mean you made things easy for the rest of us."

"The rest of us?"

"Yeah. I wasn't the only other gay guy at our school. I had a buddy on the football team that would help me out when I needed… relief."

"So, two of the assholes making my life hell were gay?"

"He had a girlfriend. I don't know if he was gay. He would just help me out sometimes."

"Because that's what friends do?" I asked him sarcastically.

"Yeah."

"Jesus!"

"What?"

I opened my mouth about to tell him how stupid he was when I stopped. He really didn't know. And how could he? How could anyone know what they don't know?

Wasn't that the purpose of a therapist, to share insights that clients wouldn't have gained any other way?

How different would my life had been if someone had helped Evan to accept himself? I probably wouldn't be the person I am today. I didn't know if I would be better or worse, but I sure would have liked to find out.

"Evan, have you ever thought about seeing someone? Like a therapist?"

"I don't need to see a therapist," he responded defensively.

"First of all, you absolutely do. I can barely think of anyone who needs to see one more."

Evan lowered his eyes. "I know."

"You do?"

"Yeah. I might be dumb. But I ain't stupid."

"So, why haven't you?"

"I don't know. But, maybe if you were willing to spend some time with me."

"Okay, that's never gonna happen, ever! There's too much that has gone on between us."

"Yeah, you're right."

"But, there are a lot of people out there who are willing to help you. There's an LGBT center in Nashville. And if going in there in person would be too much for you, there are hotlines you can call. What I'm saying is, there's a way out of what you're feeling. You don't have to hate yourself anymore."

Evan's gaze dipped. A moment of silence went by before he spoke again.

"Can I ask you something?"

"What's that?"

"Why were you so mean to me that first day? Because it really hurt."

I thought back. I didn't remember much of it. For the most part, it was just another day. Was this how he remembered all of the days he hurt me?

"I don't know. I was probably just being insecure. Or, maybe I was just being a dick," I admitted. "I was dealing with a lot back then."

Evan held out his hands in front of him and slowly pointed his fingers towards himself mirroring my gesture. He didn't do it as forcefully as I had, but I got his point.

"Can I ask you another question?"

"What?"

"Do you forgive me?"

I stared at him. Did I forgive Evan Carter, star of my nightmares and terrorizer of my youth?

"Evan, you hurt me. I'm still dealing with the scars."

"If it makes you feel any better, so am I. I wake up screaming having dreamed about what I did to you back then."

"You have nightmares about what you did to me?"

"All the time. It haunts me. I was kinda glad when you had your friend beat the shit out of me. I thought I would be able to consider us even. But, it didn't change anything."

"Which is why you came here?"

"Yeah."

"And why I've been seeing you around campus."

Evan looked away.

"And why I saw you around campus so much my freshman year?"

He looked at the ground.

"So, I wasn't going insane. That really was you."

"I just want you to forgive me."

I looked at the guy I had thought about so much throughout my life. For the first time in a long time, I saw him as human.

"Evan Carter, I forgive you," I said surprised to hear it come out of my mouth.

He got off his knees.

"Really?" He asked excitedly.

"Yea."

With a smile on his face, he threw his arms open about to hug me.

"No!" I said coldly. "I forgive you. But we aren't friends. And, you need to get help. You owe it to me and everyone else you've hurt."

I paused catching myself.

"More than that, you owe it to yourself. You don't have to feel like this and there could be a really great life waiting for you on the other side."

Evan settled himself. "I appreciate you saying that."

"I never want to see you again, Evan. Is that clear?"

He took a deep breath. "It's clear."

"Good. And, good luck," I said sincerely.

"Thank you, Kendall, for everything," he said before turning around and walking out of my life forever.

I couldn't have imagined how cathartic my conversation with Evan could have been. Watching him walk away, I felt different. Everything felt different. Never had I been surer about what I was going to do with my life. I wanted to help little boys like Evan. Intervening with them early could change their lives and the lives of everyone around them.

But, it wasn't just LGBT kids I wanted to help. There were adults. A lot of people in this world were in pain. I thought about it. Wasn't Nero one of them?

I was never meant to be with Nero. That wasn't why we had been put together. I was there to help him. I knew he was having a rough time with life. I knew he was inclined to make bad decisions. Yet, I allowed things to develop between us.

It was wrong of me. If I cared about him… if I truly cared about him, then I had to do better. If I loved him like I claimed to, then I had to make a decision for him. We couldn't be together. Not if I cared about him. And not if I'm going to help him.

I knew what his problem was and he wouldn't be having it if I hadn't stuck my nose in where it didn't belong. When I heard his mother's story, it broke my heart so it had to have devastated Nero. Someone had to tell him that he mattered to them. A lot of someones had to tell him.

Marching back to my room to come up with a plan, I got a phone call from somebody I hadn't expected.

"Quin? What's up?" I asked happy to hear from him.

"Have you seen Nero?"

"Yeah, I left him about thirty minutes ago. He had an interview with a Nashville reporter. I think he's still at the sports facility."

"I don't think he is."

"What's going on?"

"I just got a call from Titus. He walked in on him tearing apart their room and when Titus went to stop him, Nero knocked him out. He said, when he woke up,

Nero was gone. Kendall, I don't see him doing anything good."

Shit!

"Do you have any idea where he might be?" Quin pushed.

"None."

"Really? Because I was counting on you knowing something."

"I'm sorry, I don't."

As soon as I said it, an image flashed into my mind. It was of us standing at the edge of the lake. It was where he ran to when he was a kid. I don't know why I thought about it, but remembering the moment I fell in love with him wasn't helpful right now.

"Okay. Cage is trying to call him. Hopefully, he'll pick up."

"Let me know he's alright if you hear from him."

"I will," Quin said before ending the call.

This was my fault. There was the reason Professor Nandan wanted me there. I was supposed to be his support. Instead, I got lost in my melodrama bullshit. Now, he was out there somewhere hurting others and probably himself.

I again thought about our time at the lake. What had made me think of it? I wasn't sure. But, I had to get my head in the game. I had to think of where he could be. At some point, he must have shared something that would help now.

Continuing to think about it, I headed back to my room. I was kind of hoping that Cory wasn't there. I loved him, but he had been acting very weirdly ever since the cuddling incident.

I had tried to tell him that nothing that had happened was a big deal. Yea, he had an erection. What guy didn't in the morning? And yes, his erection touched my butt. Life goes on.

I was going through a hard time. I was appreciative that he was there for me. I told him that. He grunted something unintelligible and then got all twitchy. Like I said, he was being weird.

I really wished he wasn't because it would have been nice to tell him everything that had just happened. How many horror stories had I shared with him about Evan Carter? How many times had I woke him up with my screaming? Well, stop the presses. Evan and I are good now!

Okay, *we* weren't really good. But, I think *I'm* good. At least, I would be if it wasn't for what Quin told me about Nero. I had to think of what I could do to help. Maybe what he needed was an intervention. But instead of dragging him off to rehab, it could be people telling him how much they loved him. They could all, person after person, repeat that they loved him and how happy they are to have him in their life.

I stopped walking and pressed my fingers against my eyes. What that reminded me of was that I couldn't be one of those people. I could never be one of those people. I couldn't love him the way I so desperately wanted to. Not if I was going to give him the help that he so clearly needed. We can't all get what we want and the person who won't be able to get it this time is…

Kneeling before I fell to the ground, I sat on my ass and cried. These weren't like the tears I shed an hour ago. This time I knew why we weren't going to be together and it was out of love. This was how I could prove to him that I loved him, by putting his needs over mine. And these weren't just words and empty promises anymore. I knew what I needed to do… even if knowing didn't make things easier.

I sat on the ground crying things out. It was a while before I was able to get up and continue to my room. By the time I got there, I felt better. Okay, I didn't feel better, but I did feel stronger.

"Hey," I said to Cory who ended up being home.

"Hey," he said still not able to look me in the eyes.

"This is ridiculous, Cory, and has to stop. So, you had an erection. So, your erection touched my butt. Are you so insecure that you're gonna let a little homoerotic cuddling ruin our friendship? Things happen! I mean how homophobic are you?"

"Kendall, I'm not straight!" He said cutting me off.

I paused to make sure I heard what I did.

"I'm sorry, what?"

"I'm not straight. I've always suspected something was different about me. But, I've been with Kelly for so long that I didn't think it would be an issue. I didn't think I would have to deal with it. But, I can't deny it anymore. I'm not straight," he said looking at me with his big puppy dog eyes.

I stared at Cory not saying a word. A part of me was shocked by the news. Another part screamed, 'I knew it!' But, I also knew there was a certain way I was supposed to handle this. After all, wasn't he coming out to me? I was a gay guy. I was supposed to be good at this stuff.

"Aren't you gonna say anything?" He asked.

Having waited far too long to speak, I knew there was only one thing I could do. So, I walked up to him, threw my arms around him, and squeezed.

"I'll be here for you. Whatever you need," I told him meaning it.

"Thank you."

I let him go and held his shoulders in my hands.

"So, what narrative are we going with? Are we gonna say that cuddling with me turned you? Or…?" I asked with a smirk.

Cory laughed. It was good to see him smile again. At least one of us was happy.

"You wish," he said cheering up.

"I mean, if you were single, maybe."

"Oh!" Cory said suddenly becoming serious.

"But, you're not!" I reminded him. "And I'm having a crisis with the guy I was supposed to be with, but am not, apparently."

"What's going on?"

Telling Cory everything that had happened since the last time we spoke took the rest of the day. When it became dark outside and I still hadn't heard from Quin, I texted him.

'Any word yet?'

'Nothing. He didn't attend practice. Everyone's still looking.'

"This is insane. Where could he have gone?"

Thinking about it again, I drew a blank. All I could think about was looking down at him as he threw up at the mention that he could hurt me. How could someone be so tough, yet so sensitive?

I was barely able to fall asleep that night, but when I did, I kept dreaming of one location over and over again. It was of the lake. In one dream I was asking him why he had left me. In another, I had asked him why he would hurt himself. So, when I woke up, the first thing I did was call Quin.

"Did you hear from him?" Quin asked desperately.

"Maybe. I don't know. But I think I know where he is. It was somewhere he took me when I was in Snow Tip Falls."

"Cage has been looking everywhere there. He's been asking everyone."

"It's not in town. I'll tell you how to get there. But, before I do, I need you to do something. It's important. It's a matter of life and death."

Chapter 12

Nero

I sat in my truck staring at the lake in front of me. It stared back unchanging. I had been here all night. Yet, I was no closer to deciding where I was going or what I was doing next.

The first time I was here, things had quickly become clear. What I had to do was protect Mama. That meant that I had to return and become the person I did.

What about now? There was no one I had to return for. I had betrayed Kendall and he had watched me do it. I got to see how much it had hurt him. I had thought that football could be enough for me. It isn't. Yet, it was now all I had.

How could my life have turned out like this? It was just a few weeks ago that I thought I had it all. But realizing that no one ever wanted me, I saw just how much of a lie that was.

I had nothing and no one. I didn't know what was holding me back from ending it all. Starting the truck and staring the lake down in one last battle of wills, I was about to shift the truck into drive when something in my periphery moved.

My eyes flashed up to the rearview mirror. There was a truck approaching. I recognized it. It was Cage's. What was he doing here?

Before I had time to think about it, another truck appeared behind it. It was Titus's. Behind that were a few I recognized from around Snow Tip Falls. There was even one that I recognized from the football stadium parking a lot.

What the hell was going on? Of all of the places in the world, why were they here? Why now?

Turning off my engine, I got out and watched them park. Cage was the first to get out of his truck and race to me.

"Nero, we found you. We were so worried. Why the hell didn't you answer your phone? We didn't know what to think," he told me before throwing his arms around me locking me into a hug.

"I…" I stammered.

Before I could answer, Titus joined us. It was a relief to see that I hadn't killed him. Although, the bruise I left on his cheek would be hard to ignore.

I lost my strength reminded of what I had done. I really was the ultimate fucked up mistake. Look what I had done to my friend. I was an animal. One that deserved to be put down.

"Nero!" Quin said joining his boyfriend hugging me. "We're so happy you're safe."

Titus didn't get as close. Neither did Dr. Sonya or her son Cali. Dr. Tom, the local doctor, and his husband Glenn, stayed back a bit. So did Mike, the asshole I worked for as a busboy, and Claude, one of the football players from my high school team.

The familiar faces continued to pour out of their trucks until I had to pull away from my brothers.

"I don't get it. Why are y'all here?"

Cage and Quin stared at me.

"Because we were worried about you, Bro."

I had a hard time processing that. And, even if that were true,

"Dan, why are you here?" I asked one of my brother's friends who still played on the East Tennessee football team.

"Like he said. We were worried about you. And Cage said you needed our support. So, I'm here."

I looked at Cage.

"We knew you were going through something and everyone's here to help."

"How do you know I'm going through something?"

Titus stepped forward. "You weren't exactly subtle about it," he said with a painful smirk.

I tried to gather the strength to apologize to him but couldn't. Instead, I fell back onto my truck sitting on the bumper. Seated, I couldn't hold any of it back any longer. I cried. I wept for the mistakes I had made. I wept for the people I had hurt. And I wept because so many people were standing in front of me now.

How many of them had I hurt as much as Titus? Maybe I hadn't hit them. But I had never been a good student or teammate. Lord knows I was a shit employee. I could never get anything right.

"I don't understand. Why are you here?" I begged through the tears.

"Because we care about you," Cage insisted.

"Yes," Quin confirmed.

"That's why we're here," Titus said confidently.

"But you don't understand. None of you do."

"Then tell us," Cage said softly.

I scanned the faces of the more than 20 people staring at me and then leaned into Cage.

"Mama didn't want me. She only… "had" me, as a replacement for you."

"I know that's not true."

"But, it is."

"If you don't believe me, then she can tell you." Cage turned and yelled back at his truck. "Mama! She wasn't sure you'd want her here."

I watched as my mother got out of the backseat. I didn't know what I was expecting, but the woman approaching me wasn't the same one I had had to take care of for so many years. She was even different from the one who had told me about my conception. She looked stronger, more confident.

"Mama?"

As she approached, she opened her arms inviting me into them. I went. I wasn't sure when the last time was that she hugged me. She wasn't a hugging type even before her brain crashed. But I was beginning to realize that I never knew who my mother was.

"I'm so sorry, Baby. I'm sorry for so many reasons."

That was when I again lost it.

"You are the strongest man I know. The things that you have had to endure. I could never make it up to you, my son, my beautiful baby boy."

I grabbed my mother and bawled. Years of pain flooded out of me. I howled with anguish. With the gates open, there was no stopping it. She just stood there holding me. I never wanted to let her go.

I don't know how long it was before I was able to again gain control of myself. Realizing that everyone I knew was watching, I looked up embarrassed.

"I'm sorry," I said wiping my raw eyes.

"Don't be, Bro. Everyone here is someone who cares about you. There's no need to be ashamed of who you are. We all know what pain feels like. We're here for you. Whatever you need."

I looked around at the nodding heads. I didn't have the strength to figure out if what he was saying was true, so I believed him. It felt good to believe that I wasn't alone, so I did.

"Why here?" Mama asked looking around.

I looked at her and got a flash from seven years ago. My chest clenched. She must have noticed because she took my hand. I looked down at it again realizing how different she was.

"I don't know if I can tell you, Mama."

"You don't think I can handle it?"

I looked her in the eyes not wanting to tell her that I didn't.

"Nero, you have been strong for me for so long. Let me be strong for you, now. Tell me. Why here? What made you come here?"

I thought about it and then scanned the faces in front of me. There was no one there who knew who I had been or why. All they knew was that I was a kid who got into fights and had a temper. But, they didn't know about my life as my landlord's enforcer. My greatest accomplishment had been keeping my two lives separate. Maybe it was time to link the two.

"Mama, I had to do a lot of things to keep you safe," I began before telling all of them the gritty details of my life.

When my last story was told, I felt empty. I had never felt more raw. Everyone was looking at me with new eyes. I didn't know what to make of it.

The longer they stared, the less sure I became about sharing my monster. I opened my mouth to apologize for saying too much when Cage cut me off.

"I can't tell you how grateful I am that you told me that. I always knew there was a part of you that you never let me touch. I understand it now. You were trying to protect us."

"Yeah, thank you for sharing," Titus said. "So many things make sense now. I finally know who you are," he said with a smile.

"Yes, thank you for telling us," Quin said followed by a chorus of voices saying the same thing.

The only person who remained silent was the woman standing in front of me. She was staring at me blankly. I didn't know what to say to her or if I should say anything at all.

Maybe I shouldn't have told her any of what I had. It was too late now. The only question was whether or not finding out what I had done would cause her to retreat into her dream world.

As I thought about it, Mama lunged forward and threw her arms around me.

"I'm sorry. I'm so, so sorry. My baby. What did I do?"

"I don't blame you, Mama. You were sick. You needed help. I was willing to do anything I had to to keep you safe. I love you, Mama!"

"Baby, I love you so much! You are my entire world," she said silently crying.

I held my mother for as long as she needed me to. Once she let me go, I decided to bring whatever this was to an end.

"I can't tell you what it means that y'all did this for me. It blows my mind. Thank you."

Faces smiled back.

"I'm better now. I think I'll be heading home. You should too. Unless you can't get enough of the view," I said gesturing towards the haunting lake.

A few people laughed.

"I didn't think so. But, thank you for being here for me. Seriously," I said putting my hand on my heart.

"Of course," Dan said turning to head back to his truck. "Are you gonna be at practice?"

"As long as I get back in time."

"Get your ass there. Coach will throw a fit if he doesn't have his star running back for another day," Dan said with a smile.

"Whatever," I told him smiling back.

Saying goodbye to each of them took a while. I swore that I was going to catch up with Claude. Unlike most of the people in our Snow Tip Falls high school class, he went to university immediately after graduation. He told me he had moved back and that we had a lot to catch up on. I told him I was looking forward to it and thanked him again for coming.

When it was finally just me, my brothers, my mother, and Titus, I stated the obvious.

"It was like everyone I ever knew was here… except Kendall."

"He was the one who organized this," Quin said.

"What?"

"Yeah. He was the one who told us you'd be here. And, he told us that this was what you needed most."

"He did?"

"Yes."

"Then, why isn't he here?" I asked, my exhausted heart thumping painfully.

Quin looked around at everyone. As soon as he did, they drifted away. The two of us were alone. My heart pounded afraid of what was coming next.

"He said, he wouldn't have the courage to say this to you directly, so he asked me to."

"Okay," I said with building terror.

"He said that he loves you. He loves you so much that he's willing to do whatever he has to to help you. And that means that the two of you can't be together. He wants to help you. He wants to be there for you. But, it can't be as anything more than counselor/student."

Quin stared into my eyes with sympathy.

"I'm so sorry, Nero. I know that you love him. What are you gonna do?"

I stared at Quin thinking about Kendall's message. How was someone supposed to respond to that? What was I going to do now?

Chapter 13

Kendall

I stood in front of the door leading to Commons wondering if I would be able to do this. This would be the first time I spoke to Nero since arranging the intervention at the lake. Quin told me that he delivered my message and that Nero accepted it. I could tell that he had because he hadn't reached out to me since then.

Though, I was half expecting that he would. I figured that it would be to thank me. I didn't need the gratitude. It was enough to know that it had helped. But, I guess I thought he wouldn't be able to stop himself.

There was also a part of me that hoped he wouldn't respect my request. Maybe it was the romantic in me, but I was partially hoping he would refuse to keep things professional and would sweep me off my feet.

In my heart, I knew that would be the worst possible decision he could make. I could help him so much more in this capacity. So, in the end, I guess I'm glad he didn't.

But, didn't every boy want to feel wanted so badly that someone says, "The hell with all of the rules. I'll have you no matter what." I can admit that I am such a boy even if I know it's for the best that he didn't.

Taking a final deep breath, I pushed open the large metal door and entered the building. Sending the stairs, I looked around at the tables. We had agreed to grab dinner at the café and eat it while doing what would become our twice a month counseling session. I tried to come up with the most boring arrangement possible. And again, to my surprise, Nero had agreed.

Spotting him as he spotted me, I pointed towards the café telling him I would grab my food. Luckily he already had a sandwich in front of him. It would allow him to hold the table. They were hard to find at this hour. I guess that meant that he had arrived a little early.

Charging my food to my meal plan, I took my tray to his table and settled myself across the two-top from him. I tried not to think about how beautiful he was. I also tried not to think about what it was like making love to him. I tried not to think about what it felt like as he pushed into me. This was going to be harder than I thought.

"Hi," I said awkwardly.

"Hi," he said without his usual charming smile.

I knew I was supposed to be the one driving this conversation, but it had never been our dynamic. He was always the one trying to get me to talk. Everything seemed out of whack between us now. But, I was going to figure out how to make this work.

"So, Quin said that things went well by the lake. Would you agree with that?"

"Would I agree? Sure."

The silence drew out when he didn't say any more.

"Good. Do you want to share anything from the experience?"

"Like what?"

"Anything that stands out. Anything that might be helpful for me to know."

Nero thought for a second. "I told everyone the story I told you about being my landlord's enforcer."

"Really? And, how did that go over?"

"Pretty good. They thanked me for sharing it. There were a few people there who I had been a real dick to in high school and even they thanked me."

I looked at him confused. "How many people were there?"

"Twenty? Twenty-five?"

I tried not to react. I had told Quin that it was important to get as many people there as he could. But, I was picturing six or seven. Twenty was an army.

I would have given anything to see everyone or even be there. After all, I had been the one to arrange it for the man I love.

"That's excellent. I'm happy it was so successful. What about practice? How has that been going?"

Nero gave me a rundown of the trivial things he had been dealing with and then looked at me for my next question. The truth was that I didn't have anything else to ask him. I looked down at my half-eaten sandwich and wondered if I should wrap it up and take it to go.

"What about you?" Nero asked me. "How have you been? Or, am I not supposed to ask. I'm not sure what the rules are."

I thought about that. I was making things up as I went along so I didn't know what the rules were either.

"No, you can ask," I said with a tight-lipped smile.

"Then, how have you been?"

I considered what I should tell him. I certainly couldn't say how much I had been struggling since requesting we keep things professional. He certainly didn't have to hear about that.

"Oh! I saw someone unexpected recently."

"Who's that?"

"Evan Carter."

As soon as I said the name, Nero's body tensed. He went from soft puppy dog to fearsome protector in an instant.

"Don't worry, it was all good."

"It was good? How?"

"He actually found me on campus."

"I told him if he came looking for you…"

"No, Nero. Trust me. It was a good thing. Turns out, the reason he was so awful to me in high school was because he's gay too and I was forcing him to confront his sexuality before he was ready. He actually fell to his knees and begged for my forgiveness. And, it wasn't because he was scared of you. He felt that bad about it."

"The fact that you're smiling tells me that you got a kick out of it," Nero observed.

"Am I smiling?"

"A lot."

I was smiling. "Oh. Well, the experience was everything I dreamed would happen."

"I thought my beating the crap out of him was everything you dreamed of."

"Before I knew that your beating him up was an option, him on his knees begging for forgiveness was the dream. But, I don't think he would have done it if you hadn't balanced the scales a little. So, thank you again for that."

"It feels good knowing I was able to play at least a small part in your happiness," he said rediscovering his smile, as bittersweet as it was.

"You've played a large part in it," I admitted vulnerably.

"Maybe I can again?" He asked putting his heart in his hands.

God, did I want to say yes. But instead, I adverted my eyes.

"Of course," he said suddenly collecting his stuff. "Was there anything else that we needed to discuss?"

"No. As long as everything's going well with you and you haven't felt any impulses to lash out?"

"I haven't. And, I don't think I've ever been so clear about what I want and how to get it."

"Oh! Was is it that you want?"

Nero looked at me and got up. "You said that we aren't allowed to talk about it," he told me before giving me a steely gaze then walking away.

I wasn't sure what he meant by that. What did I say that we weren't allowed to talk about? Although there were things that it was clear to me we should let go of, I didn't remember placing any limits on our discussions.

I hadn't realized how hard it would be watching him walk away from me, but it was. The image of his backside stuck with me. Someone might guess it was because of his incredibly tight ass. But, it was more than that. His backside meant that he was leaving me. And the thought of being without him always sent painful throbs through my body.

As the days and weeks passed, things didn't get much easier. He and I met every other week for our sessions and to his credit, Nero kept them as professional as our first. The truth was that being with him showed me how lonely my life had been before I had met him.

Sure, Cory was great. And helping him come to grips with his new bisexual identity was fulfilling. But, with Nero had come a family and an interesting new best friend who I desperately wanted to see again. So, when I got a text from Quin inviting me to dinner, I couldn't accept it fast enough.

"How have you been?" I asked as we sat down at the Thai restaurant.

"Good! I think we're completely moved in. Finally!"

"Have you been heading up more often?"

"Unfortunately not. I was up last weekend, but I can't this weekend. By the way, we're doing a game night at my place on either Saturday or Sunday night. Would you like to come?"

I didn't have to think about it. Of course I did.

"Is Nero gonna be there?"

"He has an away game this weekend, so probably not. But it's an important game for him, so depending on which day we do it, we might have it on in the background."

I thought about it. I missed hanging out with Quin nearly as much as I missed being with Nero. At least I got to talk to Nero every two weeks. Quin had disappeared from my life.

I understood. I had drawn a line in the sand and Nero was his future brother-in-law. But the idea of spending time with him while watching Nero do what he did best was near irresistible.

"Can I let you know?"

"Sure," Quin said falling silent. He looked disappointed.

"It's not that I don't want to come. I just don't know if I should."

"Ya know, I once chose my work over Cage."

"What do you mean?"

"I grew up feeling a lot of pressure to do the right thing. For me, the right thing was to change the world with my work. To me, Cage and Snow Tip Falls didn't fit into that picture. So I chose work over Cage."

"What changed?"

"Someone wiser than me talked me out of it."

"You know our situations are different, right?"

"Of course. You believe that you have to give up being with him because it's the only way you can help him."

"It is. It is a long-accepted rule in therapy that you can't have a personal relationship with the person you trying to help."

"But you're not his therapist."

"Call it whatever you want. I'm the one who will do whatever it takes to help him be happy."

"Have you considered that the happiest he's ever been was when he was with you? I saw the way he was when the two of you were together. I've never seen him happier."

I thought back to our time in Snow Tip Falls. I had to agree with Quin. Not only was that weekend the happiest I had ever seen Nero, but it was also the happiest I had ever been.

"I really want to help him get everything he's ever wanted, Quin."

"What if everything he ever wanted was you?"

I wanted to believe what Quin was suggesting.

"I think we both know how much football means to him."

Quin looked away and nodded his head in thought.

"Do you love him, Kendall?"

"What?"

"I'm saying all these things, but I guess it wouldn't matter if you didn't love him."

What did I tell him? Of course I loved Nero. I loved him so much I ached thinking about him. Knowing that I have an appointment to see him is what gets me out of bed in the morning. It doesn't matter how far in the future it is. The fact that I will eventually get to see him allows me to breathe.

"Yeah, I love him."

"The same wise man once told me that when you're lucky enough to find love, you have to choose it."

"Haven't I, though? I've chosen his happiness over my own."

"Have you? Or, are you running from it? You haven't told me much about your past. But, is it possible that you've been hurt before and you're using professional distance as a way not to be hurt again?"

I tried not to feel what Quin was saying but the dagger of his words sank deep. I had been hurt before. Evan Carter had filled my childhood with nothing but pain and mistrust. The fog of it was so thick I could barely see beyond it.

So, was Quin right? Was I using professional distance as a way of protecting myself from getting hurt again? Was I just... scared?

Although Quin changed the topic, I thought about what he had said for the rest of the night. When we were about to leave, he reminded me about game night.

"You said Nero won't be there?"

"He has a big away game that weekend. I don't think he could be there even if he wanted to. Would you not come if he was?"

"I don't know. But, I guess it doesn't matter since he won't be. Text me when it is. I'll try to make it," I said leaving myself some wiggle room to change my mind.

Quin wasn't shy about expressing his joy. "I'm glad. You haven't met my roommate Lou yet. He's going to be there."

"Will Titus?" I asked remembering what Nero had told me about Titus and Quin's roommate.

Quin laughed. "Oh right. You know about the two of them. I don't know why those two won't just get together and get it over with."

"Lou likes him, too?"

"Who can tell with that one? I think he's too busy trying to figure out what he's missing out on to realize what he has."

"So much drama!"

"I feel like I'm living in a gay soap opera," he said with a smirk.

"Well, I'm ready for my close-up," I said knowing the role I was playing.

"I didn't mean you."

"Yeah, you did. And, that's fine. I get it."

"I just think you two could be happy together."

"Maybe we could be," I admitted realizing it for the first time. "But, how about we start with game night," I said with a smile.

By the time I left Quin, I was in a really good mood. I had missed him a lot. I couldn't wait to reconnect with everyone I had met through him and Nero.

However, a strange thing happened. As soon as I thought about Nero and me being together, I felt a clench in my chest. I hadn't felt this before. Of course, I had also never truly considered the two of us being together.

Sure, there was hardly a day when I didn't imagine having sex with him. I also thought about the warmth and safety I felt lying in his arms. But opening up and showing him my heart? Making myself vulnerable? Giving him the power to hurt me like the others had?

Maybe I had put distance between Nero and me out of fear. If that was the case, could I change things even if I wanted to? Not only would I have to fight my own resistance, but hadn't I succeeded at pushing him away. Hadn't Nero moved on?

Realizing that I might have lost him for good sent a wave of fire through me. I had really messed things up. What was I supposed to do now?

When I was back in my room, I stared at my phone. I wanted to call Nero. I needed to hear his voice. Could I, though? On the other hand, why shouldn't I?

I found his number and was about to dial it. I stopped. I couldn't. It was too much. It would be too scary.

'Good luck on your game this weekend,' I texted him instead.

His reply came immediately.

'Thanks! It's a big one.'

'You're gonna crush it. I know you will.'

There was a pause.

'If you want, I'll win it for you,' he eventually wrote.

I stared at the words. How was I supposed to respond to that? As a counselor, I knew what I should say. I should tell him that he should win it for himself. But, I didn't want to.

'Win it for me,' I wrote back before I realized what I was writing.

'Anything for you,' he replied followed by a smiley face that melted my heart.

My skin tingled rereading his words. My insides were a tornado of sensations. Fear. Joy. Apprehension. I wanted to escape into the night and run to him. I felt everything.

This was what I had been afraid of from the moment I met him. What if he pushed me away now? How would I survive it with my defenses down? I don't think I could. What was I supposed to do?

I didn't sleep for a second that night. I could barely sleep the night after that. I was exhausted and yet I wasn't tired.

It was like I had been chugging Red Bulls. My heart pounded like it would explode. The only thing that gave it any relief was when Quin texted telling me game night would be Sunday.

'Are we gonna watch Nero's game? Isn't that Saturday?'

Quin didn't write back immediately.

'We all promised not to watch it until game night Sunday. Do you promise?'

I didn't know how to respond. I wasn't a football fan, but I was a fan of Nero. Hadn't he said he was going to win the game for me? Shouldn't I at least congratulate him if he wins?

'Does Nero know you all are waiting to watch it?'

'Yes. And I told him that you would be joining us. So, do you promise?'

'As long as he knows.'

'He does.'

'Okay. I'll avoid any news about it until game night.'

I thought about Nero from the moment I woke up Saturday morning to when I thought the game would have ended.

"Did you hear about your friend's football game?" Cory said when he returned to our room.

"No! Don't tell me. I'm gonna be watching it tomorrow with Quin and Nero's friends. Since when are you into football?"

"I'm not." He stared at me weirdly before continuing. "It was just an interesting game, that's all."

"It was interesting even though you're not into football?"

"I guess," he said hesitantly. "By the way, you're probably not gonna want to leave this room if you don't want to hear anything about it."

"Seriously?"

"Yeah."

"Well, luckily my only plan is to grab something to eat at the café."

"You're not gonna want to do that either. But luckily, I'm going there now. Do you want me to bring you back something?"

"Ah… sure? Okay, what happened at this game?"

Cory stared at me with his eyes sparkling.

"Seriously, it was nothing. You'll see it tomorrow. It'll probably be more fun to find out that way. I'll bring you back something," he said dropping off his stuff and heading back out.

Although he hadn't meant to say, I was now pretty sure that East Tennessee had won. He knew how I felt about Nero. There was no way he would smile that much if the guy I was in love with had lost.

Watching Netflix on my phone, all I wanted to do was text Nero. Resisting was the hardest thing I ever had to do. The only thing that made it bearable was knowing he hadn't texted me. Since he knew I wouldn't be watching it, he knew he had to text me if he wanted me to know.

When Cory came back with my food, he was acting completely differently. He no longer seemed like he was holding in a secret. At the same time, he was clearly avoiding my eyes. Why was he being so weird?

The next morning, things weren't that different. It was nice having him get my food for me again, though. It wasn't like I loved sitting awkwardly by myself in the cafeteria. Whatever it took for me not to have to deal with that, I was fine with.

Emerging from my room only to shower, when the time came, I got ready for game night and headed out. Maybe I was being paranoid but it felt like people were looking at me. Why would people be looking at me?

Ignoring it, I put my head down and headed to Quin's. At least when I got there, everyone was acting normally. I wanted to tell them about how weird Cory was being but I was afraid to spoil the game's outcome. So, instead, I found a seat next to Quin and enjoyed the moment.

"Are we gonna play Wavelength or watch the game? If we're playing Wavelength, Lou and I will kick your asses," Titus announced with a beaming smile.

I turned to the puckish looking guy sitting next to Titus. "I don't think we've met. Kendall," I said offering him my hand.

"Lou," he said with a smile.

"Don't even think about it, Lou," Quin said quickly.

"What? I was saying hello!"

"Sure you were."

"Seriously, who do you all think I am?" He asked genuinely offended.

"Think?" Quin asked with a smile.

Lou looked at him shocked.

"Don't worry, Lou. I have your back," Titus said throwing his arm around him and giving Quin a disapproving look."

"At least someone does," he said hurt.

Quin looked at me and mouthed the word, drama. I chuckled.

When Titus and Lou became lost in conversation, I turned to Quin and whispered, "Isn't Titus on the football team?"

"He got cut a couple of games ago. Don't ask him about it. It's still a sensitive topic."

I was going to ask about Nero's team when Quin's intercom buzzed as if using Morse code.

"That's Cage," Quin said getting up and buzzing him in. "Everyone's here," he said into the intercom before opening the living room door.

Cage entered carrying a couple of pizzas. Quin kissed him.

"You said you were bringing a surprise. What is it?" Quin asked looking at him confused.

Cage looked up at me and then at the others. "One of the pizzas is pineapple."

Titus laughed. "How is that a surprise? You bring that every time."

Quin looked at Titus. "It's a surprise because I had gently suggested that he switch it to something else."

"Did you, Baby. I'm so sorry about that. I forgot."

Lou laughed. "Sure you did. The next thing you're gonna say is that you conveniently forgot to bring the hot friend you keep talking about."

"Who, Claude? Was I supposed to invite him?" Cage asked surveying the room.

Lou gave Cage the side-eye. "I'm gonna forgive you because you're cute."

I looked over at Titus. He still had his usual smile but it was much dimmer and he was looking away.

"Anyway, how about we start the football game? I'll set up Wavelength."

"I'll help you," I told Quin, already having a good time.

Quin turned on the TV. As soon as he did, the announcer mentioned Nero. I was taken by surprise.

"He's breaking records as a freshman and is nearly a sure thing to enter the draft this year," the grey-haired burly man said.

"Entering the draft and being picked high enough to get playing time on an NFL team, are two different things," the younger more athletic announcer replied.

"Well, we'll see what he has today. He is just one of many young hopefuls wanting tonight's game to be their introduction onto the national stage."

"So, this is a *really* important game for Nero?" I asked Quin not having realized how big of a game it was.

"It's his first chance at getting national attention. If he enters the draft, he'll still have to go through tryouts where they'll see how fast he runs and all of that. But if he plays well here, he'll show everyone how he performs under pressure. That counts a lot," Quin explained.

Once Quin told me that, I was hooked. Sure, I helped set up and then played the board game, but most of my focus was on the TV. When the teams exited the tunnels, my heart thumped.

"That's him. It's Nero," I told everyone when they showed him warming up on the sidelines.

My God was he beautiful. I had seen him in his football uniform, but only from the nosebleed seats of the university's stadium. Seeing him close up, I had to bend over to hide how happy I was.

The first time he stepped onto the field I could barely breathe I was so nervous. It didn't take long for him to get into position and fall back. In a second he was running with the ball in his hand. I hadn't even seen the handoff from the quarterback. And running into a wall of two-hundred-pound men, somehow he found a crack.

"Oh my god!" I said springing to my feet. "He's got it! He's got it!" I said as he spun past one defender after another.

Eventually, he was running in an open field. He passed the twenty-yard line, then the ten. There was only one defender left in view. That one was sure to take Nero down before he reached the goal line.

The opponent dove. Nero jumped. As if he were an acrobat, Nero flipped over his opponent's head and somersaulted into the end zone. It was the most amazing thing I had ever seen.

"He did it!" I screamed with excitement.

Everyone around me cheered. I had never felt more elated. I felt drunk without having had a drink. I wanted more of what I had just seen. Having avoided football my whole life, I hadn't realized how thrilling it could be.

There was no way I could pay attention to the board game after that. The only two people who could were Titus and Lou. Eventually, they started playing a game on their own. The rest of us sat glued to the TV as if our lives depended on it. I wondered how much of mine did.

Nero had said that he would win this game for me. What would it mean if he won it? What would happen if he got drafted? Wouldn't that mean he would have to move? And would he want to be with a guy while playing professional football? It wasn't exactly the most open-minded sport.

Although they were all legitimate concerns, I didn't have time to think about them now. Because as amazing as the first play of the game was, there were a lot more that followed. The football didn't always end up in Nero's hands. But, when it did, it was an automatic touchdown. It was the most incredible thing I had ever seen.

I wasn't alone. The announcers couldn't stop talking about it. They called him a star in the making. He was. And with every play, I fell more in love with the guy who had already changed my world.

At halftime, Nero's team was up by twelve. The announcers said that Nero had broken the record for most yards run in a half. I was so proud of him that my heart hurt. I could have cried just thinking about it.

When the second half started, Nero picked up where he left off. Spinning, diving, dodging, he was practically dancing on the field. No one could stop him.

By the end, the announcers said that he had shattered every record in college football history. So when they cut to a postgame interview with him, I had to wipe the tears from my cheeks.

"Nero Roman, you just broke the NCAA records for yards run, connected passes, and touchdowns in a game, and you did it as a freshman. Your name will be cemented in college football history as one of the greatest ever. I have to ask, what inspired this performance?"

Nero looked at the woman interviewing him with a light in his eyes. It was like he had been waiting for this moment.

"Love. Love inspired this."

"Your love for football."

"No," he said with a smile. "Football is great. But I told someone that I would come out here and do everything I could to win this game for them. So I did.

"Kendall, everything I did, I did for you. I know you think we shouldn't be together. But I want you to know that I'm gonna do anything and run through any line I have to to be with you. Because, you make me better. You make me wanna be better. And, when I get you back in my life, you're gonna make me the happiest person on the planet.

"I love you, Kendall. I have from the first moment I saw you. And nothing anyone will do or say will ever change that," he said, his eyes tearing up as he stared into the camera at me.

"Well, there you have it, Frank. A historic game by a freshman all done not for the love of the game, but the love of a girl. Back to you…"

Nero reached over and pulled the microphone back to him cutting her off.

"Kendall's a guy. The person I won this game for is a guy. I just wanted everyone to know that. And, I could never love anyone more."

The interviewer looked at him dumbstruck. It took a moment before she turned back to the camera and said, "There you have it. A game won for love. None of us have ever seen anything like it. Back to you, Frank."

I stared at the TV stunned. I was speechless. It took a moment to realize that tears were rolling down my cheeks. Looking around, I wasn't alone. The only one not crying was Cage. He was smiling and looking at me like he knew something I didn't. That was when he got up, walked to the door, and opened it.

"Now for my surprise," Cage said revealing Nero standing in the doorway with a bouquet of roses.

"Nero! You're here!" I said springing to my feet.

"I heard you were gonna be at game night. I couldn't stay away," he said with a smile.

My heart melted. I couldn't speak.

Nero stepped into the room. With him standing in front of me, everyone stared at us.

"I bought these for you," he said handing me the beautiful flowers. This did not help my crying.

"But, you're the one who won the game. Shouldn't I be giving you flowers?"

"Maybe if this was about the game. But it isn't."

"What is this about?"

"Did you hear what I said in my interview after the game?"

I tightened my lips and nodded nervously.

Nero opened his mouth to speak and then looked around at everyone.

"You think we could have some privacy?"

"Sure, bro," Cage told him. "Why don't we go grab some ice cream?" He said to everyone else in the room. "You want us to bring any back?"

Nero turned to me gazing into my eyes. I was mesmerized.

"We'll bring some back," Cage confirmed before heading out and leaving us alone.

With everyone gone, Nero took my hand and led me to the couch. Turning off the TV, he rested my roses on the table and took both of my hands in his.

"I meant what I said, Kendall. No one has ever done more for me than you have. You arranged for everyone in my life to find me and tell me how much I mean to them? Who does that? You are the most incredible guy I've ever met. I would be a fool if I didn't do everything I could to have you in my life."

I opened my mouth to speak, but he cut me off.

"And I know what you're gonna say. You think that the only way you can help me is by keeping things professional between us. But if I have to choose between having a football career and you, I choose you. If it's between millions of dollars and you, I choose you.

There's nothing I would choose over you. And if you just gave us a chance, I promise, I'll never let you regret it.

"I'll work every day to make you as happy as you've already made me. And I don't care what anyone thinks about us or says. I love you. I will always love you. I want to be with you. And, I'm standing here hoping to god that you'll say yes."

I stared at him. I could only say one word.

"Yes."

"Yes, you'll be with me?" He asked his face beaming.

"Yes, I love you. Yes, to all of it," I said needing him.

"I can't believe it. I..."

That was when I kissed him. The feeling of his lips on mine turned my brain into melted caramel. My head spun. I needed to be a part of him. And, as if reading my thoughts, Nero gripped the back of my head and parted my lips.

Our tongues danced together. It was crackling flashbulbs. I was alive for the first time. Warmth wafted through me, but I wanted more. So, when he slipped his hand under my shirt and found my flesh, I moaned with pleasure.

Driven by my yearning desires, Nero stripped my chest bare. Pushing me back onto the couch, he took control. Pinning my wrists above me, he turned my chin and nibbled on my ear. I could barely breathe from the sensation.

His thick tongue touched my canal. It electrified me. I could hear every sound of him. It was driving me wild. My chest was heaving. I couldn't stop it. So, when he kissed down my body pausing on my nipple, my legs danced begging for more.

With his hands now gripping the back of my arms, he took my nip in his teeth. I was as sensitive as fuck and he was biting it. It hurt but the pleasure of it made me purr.

Finally when he locked his jaw not seeming like he would let go, I struggled against his powerful grip. Only then did he continued his trail of kisses down my body. I felt the pleasure of relief.

The world around me was cold. His lips were warm. I could feel the tip of his nose and his breath. That was hot. His heat enveloped me further robbing me of my will. So, when he reached the waist of my pants and teased releasing my button, I wanted him so badly, I could snap.

Rubbing his angular cheeks against my hard cock, he teased me. I tensed unable to do anything else. He pushed back on it telling me he was there.

I wanted more than that, though. So, when he undid my pants, I ached to feel his flesh on mine. With him quickly stripping me naked, I didn't have to wait long.

Looking up at him, I felt vulnerable as he examined me. He was looking at me like I was his. His look was right. I was willing to do anything he wanted me to.

Standing next to the couch, he removed his shirt. Nero had the chest of a god. His rounded pecs quivered and his rippling abs glistened. His arms were brick houses and his shoulders were broader than any bridge.

I couldn't believe that this guy was mine. He was the most beautiful person I had ever seen. And when I saw the outline of what crossed the length of his pants, I swallowed. He was about to dominate me with it and I wanted him to. I wanted to take all of him until he had nothing left to give.

So, when he unbuttoned his pants and climbed between my legs, my cock danced. He was taking me in his mouth like he once had. His insides were a furnace. I burned for him.

With him gently massaging my balls, his tongue rode the lines of my dick. Tracing it up, he continued onto the ridge of my head. I could barely contain myself as he did it. I had never felt more sensitive in my life.

I could only stand it for a few seconds before I reached down gripping his shaggy blond hair. He must have known I was ready to blow. That was when he released my cock and grabbed the back of my thighs. Folding my hairless legs onto my chest, his tongue pushed between my cheeks.

Pressing against my button, he forced himself in me. It felt glorious. He was only preparing me, though. And when he slathered something onto me that made my hole open, he took his place on top of me leaning down kissing me.

It was as he nibbled on my bottom lip that I felt the tip of his cock pushing into me. I had remembered how big he was, but I had forgotten how it felt entering. As much as I stretched, I needed to stretch more. I groaned and twitched feeling his girth.

When my opening snapped around his head, it was a mercy as much as it was a gift. It was electric. I looked up desperately catching my breath. He gave me my moment to breathe. When he began again, I was ready.

"Ahhhh!" I moaned as I swallowed the full length of him.

In every way, he was a god. Beneath him, I was a pig spinning on his oversized spit. And when he reached the end of me and slowly pulled himself back, my toes stretched knowing what to expect.

Fucking gently to start, it didn't take long until he was riding me like a bronco. It felt fantastic. My chin pointed to the sky needing even more of him. And when he took hold of my cock and stroked me as he fucked, I grabbed his back and rode him to orgasm.

"Yeeeeeaaaaahhh!" I screamed as a powerful sensation ripped up my inner thigh and tore through my balls.

Nero thrust forward as both of us exploded. I was cumming all over the place. Nero's cum filled me.

Pinned to the couch, I felt like the flinching would never stop. As if my finger was in a socket, the slightest movement sent me twitching again. Nero didn't seem much better. He looked as scared to move as I was for him to do it. Nero had given me all of the greatest things in my life and this night turned out to be another of them.

Still catching my breath, I looked up searching for his eyes. I found them looking down at me.

"I love you," he said before I got the chance.

"I love you, too," I told him meaning it with every part of my being.

With those words, my teeth rattling spasms stopped. He was able to slip his still hard cock out of me and allow my legs to fall. I was expecting him to lie on top of me but as if I was weightless, he picked me up, switched places, and rested me on his chest.

There was nowhere in the world I would rather have been. Nero was my home. He was my protector. I was willing to do anything I had to to keep him. And I knew he would do the same.

I loved Nero with everything I had in me. And I knew I was going to love him until my dying day. Sure, we were destined to have some rough patches especially with him coming out right before the NFL draft. But there was no question about it, in the end, the two of us were going to live happily ever after.

Epilogue

Nero

Getting to draft day turned out to be a lot more complicated than I thought it would be. But sitting in the convention center with everyone I loved around the table, it was worth it.

Were the hits I got during games harder than they were before I declared my love for Kendall on national television? Some were. I also had to deal with a few more slurs. But I, and my team, got revenge the best way we knew how. We rolled through the rest of the season without dropping a game and we won our first national championship since Cage led them to the same.

That only made things a slight bit easier when it came to dealing with prospective NFL teams. I got far fewer invitations to pre-draft workouts than anyone else would with my prospect grading. I had a 7.1. That's insanely high for a running back. Yet, only seven teams worked me out. That wasn't a good sign.

Every outlet was saying my declaration of love for a guy had destroyed my chances of finding a team. I didn't care. Whatever I got, it was going to be more than I had before my brother and his incredible boyfriend entered my life.

Before him, I was hosting fight clubs for money and working as a busboy. Because of my man-loving brother, I got a scholarship, found the love of my life, and had a chance at a career in professional football. It was now looking like it was going to be as a video coordinator or something. But as long as I had my family and Kendall by my side, I didn't care.

I looked over at the love of my life. He was sitting beside me dressed in a tuxedo. God, did he look hot. How could anyone not see why I fell in love with that man?

Reaching for his hand, I took it and kissed it. He smiled reminding me once again about the only important thing.

"For the first pick in this year's NFL draft…," the football commissioner said before reading the name off of a card. "Todd Percy."

"A quarterback, imagine that?" I said to Cage who gave a sarcastic chuckle. "That could have been you."

"I'm happy right where I am, thank you very much," he said intertwining his fingers with Quin's.

Maybe Cage had it right all along. He had chosen a life with Quin over all of this draft bullshit. And working as a high school football coach in Snow Tip Falls, he couldn't be happier. Seriously, I didn't know anyone happier than my brother. Not even Titus and it was like he put drugs in his morning coffee.

Staring at Titus I decided that no matter what happened today, I was going to do whatever I had to help him find his love. After I sucker-punched him like I did and he still showed up for my intervention, he deserved at least that much.

He was the best friend I had ever had. I was going to help him get Lou. That was who would make him happy, wasn't it? Even if he still wouldn't admit it or what he was.

My agent's phone rang snapping me out of my thoughts. It was sitting on the table in front of him. Looking over, he looked back at me and picked it up.

"For the second pick in this year's NFL draft…," the commissioner said picking up the envelope in front of him.

"Absolutely," my agent said with a look of shock on his face. He ended the call and stared at me. "I don't believe it."

"What?" I asked confused.

"Nero Roman," the commissioner said calling my name.

"That was the team that just drafted you. You just got drafted 2nd overall in this year's NFL draft," he told me not clearing up my confusion.

"Nero, you just got drafted to the NFL," Kendall said grabbing my face and kissing me.

I didn't understand what Kendall was talking about. My agent had told me to not expect to go earlier than the later rounds. Besides, running backs didn't go second in the draft. It didn't happen.

"Nero, get your ass up there. You just went 2nd in the draft," Cage yelled beaming.

I was stunned. I couldn't move. I looked over at my mother. She looked so beautiful in her dress. She had tears in her eyes and she clapped for me.

"Nero, you have to go on stage," Kendall reminded me finally getting me to move.

Still in a daze, I stood up. My wobbling legs almost collapsed beneath me. I fought to keep myself together. I wasn't about to fumble the play now.

Approaching the stage I realized that my life was about to exceed my wildest dreams. Not only did I have a family and an insane career, I had someone I would love until the end of time.

I really was going to do whatever I had to to make Kendall happy. I loved him with all of my heart. And as I stepped onto stage feeling the bright lights shine down on me, all I could feel was gratitude.

The only thing missing was having a father to share it with. Maybe now that I was about to be rich and famous, I would figure out a way to have that too.

Either way, I was grateful for my life. I had it all. And Kendall and I were definitely about to live happily ever after.

The end.

*****
Sneak Peek:
Enjoy this Sneak Peek of 'Serious Trouble':

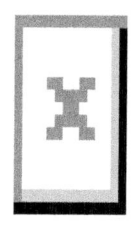

Serious Trouble
(M/M Romance)
By
Alex McAnders

Copyright 2021 McAnders Publishing
All Rights Reserved

Swoon-worthy guys; twisting story; crackling sexual tension

CAGE
With NFL scouts watching my every move, the last thing I should be thinking about is Quinton Toro, my awkwardly sexy, genius tutor who makes me think naughty thoughts. I might fantasize about everything about him at night, but I've worked too hard for too long to slip up now.

But if it came down to having him or a career in the NFL, which would I choose? The answer should be obvious, right? Then why can't I get the way he looks at me out of my mind?

I might be in trouble.

QUINTON
The problem with falling in love for the first time is that it makes you do crazy things like think you have a shot with the drop-dead gorgeous quarterback, who is not only focused on going pro, but has a girlfriend.

He is the one who insists we spend time together. That's got to mean he likes me, doesn't it? Why can't I figure this out?

And, how is he going to feel when he learns how much trouble comes with being with me? The only thing I can hope is that we can figure out a way to be together. But could love overcome all of that?

Note: This book is a part of the author's 'Love is Love Collection', meaning that it is available as a spicy romance in 'My Tutor', a wholesome romance in 'Going Long', a steamy wolf shifter romance in 'Son of a Beast', and a Male/Male romance in 'Serious Trouble'.

*****

Serious Trouble
I'm falling in love with Quin. I can't deny it. Even as I lie in the morning light not getting nearly enough sleep, all I could think about was how I could touch him like I did last night.

When I heard him place his hand on the bed between us, I sent out my hand in search of his. I didn't know if I should or if he would want me to, but I couldn't stop myself. I need Quin. I ache to be with him. I feel like I would go crazy without him. And to be so close without being able to wrap my arms around him was torture.

I was about to relieve myself of the painful agony when I shifted and something buzzed. When it did, I realized I was still half asleep because it woke me up. I knew the sound. It was my alarm clock. I had forgotten to turn it off.

It was probably more accurate to say that I wasn't foolish enough to turn it off. Ever since I had met Quin, getting eight hours were impossible. Even if I was in bed in time to do it, alone in the darkness was when I thought about him the most. So to have him here now was like a dream come true.

The alarm buzzed again. Oh right, the alarm. I didn't want it to wake up Quin.

Instead of letting it ring like I usually had to, I popped open my eyes and figured out where I was. I was on the right side of the bed. The alarm clock was on the left. I had to reach over Quin to get it.

Not thinking about it, I straddled the guy beneath me and hit the off button on the clock. With it off, I realized where I was. Although our bodies weren't touching, I was hovering above him. I froze and looked down. He was on his back facing up.

My God, did I want to bend down and kiss him. I was right there. He was so close. And then he opened his eyes.

I stared at him, caught. He smiled, or was it a blush?

"Good morning," he said in a raspy morning voice.

Looking at him, I relaxed.

"Morning," I said getting one more good look at him and then rolling back to my side of the bed. "Sorry about that," I told him.

"No, I liked it," he said smiling ear to ear.

"You liked the alarm?"

"Oh, I thought you meant…" He blushed again. "It was fine. Does that mean we have to get up? It's so early."

"I have to get to practice. It's a long drive."

"Okay," he said squirming his body adorably.

Watching him settle, I was about to get up when I noticed something. I had a serious morning wood situation going on. Sure, I was only too happy to show him my hard dick last night. But, I was so turned on by being with him that I had lost all inhibition.

After a night's sleep, as short as it was, I wasn't so bold. Yeah, I was still as turned on as all get out. But, we weren't getting into bed. We were leaving it. That made a difference.

"We could sleep a little while longer, right?" Quin asked facing me, his gorgeous eyes begging for me to hold him.

"You can, but I have to get up. The bowl game's on Saturday. This is our last full practice before it. I can't be late."

"Fine," Quin said disappointed.

Staring into his eyes I tried to think of the next time I could get him back here.

"Do you want to come to the game? Have you ever been?"

"You want me to come to your game?" He asked with a smile.

"Yeah. Why wouldn't I?"

"I don't know. I thought it might be your manly space or something."

"Manly space?"

"You know, a place for your girlfriend and all of your football friends to meet and do football things."

"First of all, the stadium seats 20,000 people. There's room for everyone. Second of all, Tasha hasn't been to one of my games in I don't know how long. You should come. That way you can see what all the fuss is about."

"I can see what all of the fuss is about from here," he said making my heart melt.

Read more now

Sneak Peek:
Enjoy this Sneak Peek of 'Hurricane Laine':

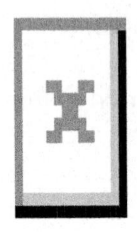

Hurricane Laine
(MMF Bisexual Romance)
By
Alex McAnders

Copyright 2020 McAnders Publishing
All Rights Reserved

A cocky billionaire, his selfless best friend, and the curvy woman neither can resist, fall into a sizzling MMF bisexual romance. Fake boyfriends, first time gay experiences, and heart-aching love follow.

JULES
Jules just got a job offer and it could not have come at a better time. Days away from ending up on the streets, she has a chance encounter with Laine, a forgotten college

classmate who offers her a weird proposal. If she pretends to be his girlfriend for a few weeks, she and her mother can keep their home.

But, why would Laine, who has become richer than god, need someone to pretend to be his girlfriend? And why would he reach into the past and ask her?

LAINE
Laine breaks things. Companies, markets, hearts, nothing is safe once he sets his sights on them. That's what made him a billionaire and why everyone worships the ground this cocky ass walks on.... That is, everyone except for one man. And for Laine, that one man is the only person who matters.

REED
Unlike Laine, his long-time best friend, Reed couldn't care less about money. In fact, after college, while Laine was becoming a corporate raider, Reed moved to a small island in the Bahamas to run an after school program for less privileged kids.

His is a quiet life... that is, except for when Laine comes to visit. So, when Laine invites Reed to stay with him on Laine's private island telling him that he will be bringing a guest, Reed braces himself for what could follow. But, as much as he prepares himself, he could never guess what Laine would do next, and how much it would change their feelings for each other.

'Hurricane Laine' is a steamy bisexual romance with as many laughs as twists and turns. Loaded with enough MM, MFM, and MMF scenes to make your toes curl, it will leave you satisfied with its not-to-be-missed HEA ending.

*****
Hurricane Laine

It was as the tears made their way to my eyes that I looked around and saw someone I truly never expected to see. It was a guy I knew from college. At least I think it was. That was approaching ten years ago. And it wasn't anyone I was friends with, but I certainly saw him around campus.

We had both gone to a small, mid-western college. The school wasn't big enough to not at least recognize everyone's face. What were the odds of running into him in a coffee shop in the middle of the day in Calabasas?

Now, here's the tricky part. I recognize him, but I don't remember his name. Here's the other thing. I have put on a few pounds since college. I was never really a thin girl, so those few pounds have tipped the scales for me.

Back then I could have considered myself to be "solid". Now, I'm… how would I say this so that I'm not being horrible to myself? Now I'm pleasantly plump.

So, with all of that in mind, do I even bother striking up a conversation? What would be the point? It wasn't like we were friends.

On the other hand, I don't remember him being this good looking. It wasn't like he was a part of the sweatsuit brigade in college, but the tailored shirt he was wearing was hanging on him like a bad habit. He's the type of guy who, if I were in a better state of mind, would make me think of sex. That's worth fumbling through a forgotten name.

As to the extra 50 pounds, couldn't I tell him that it wasn't mine and I was just holding it for a friend? Sure I could. He'd believe that, right? Besides, it's not like my life could get any worse.

"I'm sorry," I said grabbing the good looking guy's attention. When he looked at me, he had this steely look in his eyes that, if I were in a better state of mind, might have made my down-below quiver. "Do I know you?"

The good looking man flashed a good looking smile. "I don't know. Do you know me?"

He said that like he was famous or something. Wait, did I actually go to school with him or do I just recognize him from TV? Freakin' Calabasas!

"No, we went to school together, didn't we? Beloit College?"

The man's face dropped recognizing the name. He stared at me trying to figure out what was going on. It took him a second, but soon his smile returned.

"Wait, yes. Yes, I know you. You used to live in… What was that dorm closest to the gym? It was our senior year," he said excitedly.

"Haven. Yeah, it was Haven. It was our senior year. You got it," I said feeling a glimmer of hope remembering a time when my life was so full of possibilities.

"That's right, Haven," he agreed with a smile. "Laine," he said offering me a wave from two tables away."

"Jules."

"That's right, Jules," he said as if he recognized my name.

Laine stared at me for a moment with a pleasant smile on his face and gestured for permission to come over.

"Please," I told him welcoming the company.

"So, Jules, what have you been up to? What are you doing in Calabasas? Do you live here?"

Here was the tricky part. What was I supposed to tell him? In these types of situations, aren't you supposed to humblebrag about the great things going on in your life? So, what was that for me? I could tell him that I recently found $10 in a pants pocket, but I didn't want to make him feel *that* jealous.

"Honestly, not much," I told him instead. "I was up in Seattle for a while. But a family situation brought me back here."

"Are you from here?" Laine asked getting better looking by the second.

"Yeah. Not Calabasas, but Southern California."

"And, where do you work? What do you do?"

He had to ask me that, didn't he? It was such an L. A. thing to ask. I didn't have the energy to blow smoke up his ass. It had already been a long day, so I told him the truth.

"I don't work anywhere, actually."

"Oh, are you married?"

I laughed. I hadn't even dated anyone since moving back here. My lady bits have already twice filed for unemployment.

"No. It's just that I've been looking for something temporary because I don't know how long my "family situation" will last, and the agency I was working through can't seem to get their act together," I said deciding it was better to blame my situation on corporate.

"Oh, okay," he replied with quickly diminishing interest. Freakin' L. A.!

"But, how about you? What have you been up to? You look like you've done well for yourself."

This was what got his focus back on me. Who would have guessed that a guy would want to talk about himself?

"Actually, I'm doing very well. I own an investment firm."

"Really?" I asked suddenly understanding what he meant by "very well".

"Yeah. After college I moved to New York to work for one of the big banks. I shorted a couple of stocks right before the great recession and then took home a fortune," he said with a million-dollar smile.

"So, when the economy was crashing?" I asked him.

"I was raking it in."

"Huh," I said as I began to consider the morality of how he made his money.

"But, don't mistake me for those asshole bankers packaging those toxic mortgages. That wasn't me."

"No, you just made money by betting on those banks to fail."

"Actually, it was by betting on them being too big to fail," he said with another smile.

It had been a long time since I had thought about back then. We were just recent graduates entering an about to be devastated job market. It wasn't something I had the energy to think about now.

"So, are you married?" I asked him trying to cut to the good bits.

"No. Not married," he told me flatly.

"Special someone?"

"Nope. Nothing."

"How?" I asked sounding like I was flirting… because I was.

"Who knows," he said with a charming smile.

Yeah, that told me everything I needed to know. He wasn't married because he didn't want to be. Clearly, he was the type that liked to keep his options open. If today was going to end in sex, I would have to remember that. Not that it was…

"I see," I said returning his smile.

"It's funny that you asked me about that," he said seeming like he wanted me to probe.

"Why?"

Laine leaned back in his seat and looked away. "You ever get yourself in a weird situation, that you don't know how you ended up in?"

"Laine, you don't know how often. I live in that state."

Laine chuckled. "Then maybe you can relate. I'm heading down to the Bahamas in about a week…"

"Nope, can't relate," I said cutting him off. He chuckled again.

"I'm heading down in about a week and I'm going to be hanging out with a friend."

"Sounds nice."

"Yeah, but I might have told the friend a bit of an exaggeration."

"What's that?"

"I told him that I was dating someone and that I would be bringing them."

"Why would you tell him that?" I asked confused.

"I don't know. He's just a guy that makes me feel… There are some people who always make you feel bad about yourself no matter how well you're doing. That's him."

Damn, how rich does his friend have to be to make a successful investment banker feel bad about himself?

"I think I know something about how that feels," I told him genuinely relating.

"Yeah, well, that's him. And, in order to not look like a total loser, I have to find someone to go with me and pretend to be my fiancé."

"Your fiancé?"

"Yeah, I know," he said lowering his head and rubbing his eyebrows in frustration.

"I gotta say, Laine, you've gotten yourself into quite a dilemma. So, are you gonna tell him the truth?"

"Oh, god no. I can't do that."

"Why not?"

Laine paused for a moment as something flashed through his mind. "I just can't do that."

"So, what are you gonna do?"

"I have to find somebody."

"You have to find someone to go to the Bahamas with you. Yeah, good luck with that," I joked.

"It's not as easy as you think," he protested.

"Really? You can't find somebody to go to the Bahamas with you?"

"No. I can't."

"I find that hard to believe."

"I can prove it," Laine said confidently.

"How?"

"Like this. Jules, would you like to go to the Bahamas with me and pretend to be my fiancé?"

"Oh, I would love to but can't. I have to work."

"See!" He said triumphant.

"Okay, I see what you mean. But the only reason I can't do it is because I have to work. Believe me, if I didn't, I would absolutely do it. I can't tell you how much I need a trip to the Bahamas right now."

"What, the family thing?" He asked becoming more serious.

"It's a money thing. I really need to work right now. I mean, I'm not gonna get into it, but I really need the money."

So you know that feeling when a suuupper rich, suuupper handsome guy is staring at you with a twinkle in his eye that makes you want to throw yourself at him like a rug? Well, that might be what's going on now.

"Why are you staring at me like that?" I asked him.

"The only thing stopping you from helping me out is money?"

"Yeah. I don't know what world you live in. But, in my world, it's a big thing."

"I'm sure. But it's something I have," he said starting to beam with confidence.

I wasn't sure how I felt about where he was going with this. "What are you suggesting?"

"How much would get you out of your "family situation"?"

"How much? Geez, I don't know. Probably more than you have."

Laine twisted his head in doubt. God was this guy cocky. How much money did he have? My family situation could have been in the millions.

"Give me a number," he said making me question what the hell was happening.

Steadying myself I looked at Laine again. How much did I remember about him from college? Not much. I think I do remember him being a little full of himself back then, too. I really didn't interact with him, but I was starting to remember female friends who did. If I remembered correctly, he was a bit of a man whore.

And, didn't I have a girlfriend who came crying to me about him? Was that about Laine or someone else? It was such a long time ago. It's hard to remember.

Whoever it was about, it had been ten years. People change. Situations change. More importantly than all of that, *my* situation had changed. And here was a guy asking me how much money I needed to get out of the hole I'm in. What do I tell him?

If his offer was real, I certainly didn't want to scare him off by saying a number that was too high. At the same time, he was bragging about having a lot of money. Why shouldn't I at least be honest?

"$200,000."

"$200,000?" He asked with a broad smile.

"Yeah. There are medical expenses involved and a student loan that…"

"Deal," he said cutting me off.

"What?" I asked sure that I had misunderstood him.

"I said it's a deal. I'll do it. If you come with me to the Bahamas and pretend to be my fiancé, I'll pay you $200,000."

I was stunned.

Read more now

*****

Follow me on TikTok @AlexAndersBooks where I create funny, fun book related videos:

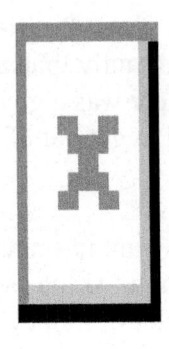

Printed in Great Britain
by Amazon